JOSHUA'S
FAMILY

JOSHUA'S
FAMILY

Joseph F. Girzone

DOUBLEDAY

New York   London   Toronto   Sydney   Auckland

PUBLISHED BY DOUBLEDAY
Copyright © 2007 by Joseph F. Girzone
All Rights Reserved

Published in the United States by Doubleday,
an imprint of The Doubleday Broadway Publishing Group,
a division of Random House, Inc., New York.
www.doubleday.com

DOUBLEDAY and the portrayal of an anchor with a dolphin are registered
trademarks of Random House, Inc.

Library of Congress Cataloging-in-Publication Data
Girzone, Joseph F.
Joshua's family / Joseph F. Girzone.—1st ed.
p. cm.
1. Joshua (Fictitious character)—Fiction.   I. Title.
PS3557.I77J69 2007
813'.54—dc22
2006034537
ISBN 978-0-385-51714-0

PRINTED IN THE UNITED STATES OF AMERICA

1   3   5   7   9   10   8   6   4   2

First Edition

JOSHUA'S
FAMILY

I

I T WAS JUST AN ORDINARY HOUSE, THOUGH NOW falling apart from lack of love. It was located on a back street in a village called Shadybrook. The house was old, that is, to a child's way of thinking. Actually, it was hardly fifty years old, which to an older person was rather new since older people are so used to one-hundred or two-hundred-year-old houses. To the people who had just moved in, it must have seemed like a dream house, even though it was run-down and shabby looking, with paint peeling off the outside and weeds running wild all around the grounds. Some might just say it was dilapidated.

Rumor had it that the family was allowed to live there free if they agreed to fix it up and paint the whole house inside and out, and take care of the front and back yards. The day they moved in, the whole village was curious, and all during the day neighbors casually walked down the street to catch a glimpse of what the newcomers were like. One of the most curious was only a young girl, not quite ten years old.

It turned out the new family were poor people, though there was a certain dignity about them. The father and mother seemed gentle; their young boy appeared to be ten or eleven, though he could have been a little older. They were dressed in simple clothes that looked well worn. The father looked older than his wife; he might be in his thirties. He had a kind face, but one could tell he had a lot of cares, as if his life was not too easy. The mother, looking younger, was maybe in her late twenties. She was very pretty; in fact, quite beautiful, with sallow skin, warm penetrating brown eyes, and long, naturally wavy brown hair gathered in the back and held together by a leather knot.

Across the street from the house, a curious little girl was watching as they moved the few pieces of furniture they had into their new home. The mother looked up and her eyes smiled at the girl. The girl smiled back and gave a shy wave of hello with her hand. The girl would never forget the beautiful smile on the woman's face. She fell in love with her immediately. No one had ever smiled at her with such love. It was as if the woman had known all about her and was telling her she liked her.

That meant so much to a girl who had little love in her life. Her father and mother were very busy doing their own things, and the girl always felt alone and, sometimes, as if she were unwanted and in the way. The look on the face of this pretty lady told her something very different. This was someone who understood and cared. The girl had a happy feeling that she and the lady would become friends.

The boy paid no attention to the girl at all. He was busy helping his father. He was a good-looking boy, with curly dark brown hair, and he was strong. He had no trouble lifting things that were quite heavy. Even though his father tried to help him, he insisted on doing it by himself. The girl heard him telling his father, "Don't you know I am a big boy now, Abba?" She did not know what "Abba" meant. Was that his father's name? Hearing his mother calling her son, the girl now knew the boy's name was Joshua.

When Joshua went into the house, the girl left and walked down the street with a happy smile as she thought about how the lady had smiled at her. She felt all warm and happy inside. As soon as she walked into the house, her mother noticed the change in her. The ordinarily sad look was gone.

"Marguerite, I saw you skipping up the front walk. When you went out you seemed sad. Now you seem so happy. What changed you, child?"

"Mommy, that new family moving into that old house down the street, the lady, the mother, smiled at me. I could tell she likes me."

"Now listen! We don't know those people, who they are, or what they are like. They may *not* be nice people for all we know."

"But, Mother, they seem so nice. They are all nice to each other and help each other. The boy doesn't even have to be told what to do. He just goes ahead and does things to help his father. He calls his father 'Abba.' That's a funny name. And, Mother, the boy is so strong. I heard his mother calling him Joshua. That's his name."

"I don't want you getting close to those people, Marguerite. There are already rumors flying around about them. They're poor, and we don't know anything about them. They may be nice people, but they may be lazy. It's hard to be poor today if you have any kind of ambition. So I don't want you hanging around there."

Marguerite always listened to her mother, and that is what she did then, but she knew she had to see those nice people again. She felt so happy just being near them. And she knew they were nice in spite of what people were rumoring about them already when they didn't even know them.

As much as she tried to obey her mother, she could not avoid meeting them at the most unexpected times, as if the encounters had been planned: like the time her mother sent her to the Shadybrook grocery store to buy some baking powder so she could bake a cake. The baking powder was right on the shelf where the pretty lady was putting a bag of flour into her basket. Marguerite tried not to talk to her, but she could not help just looking at her. She was so beautiful. The woman turned and looked at Marguerite and smiled, just the way she had when the girl saw her the first time.

"My name is Miriam," she said as she held out her upturned hand. She had never seen anyone offer to shake hands like that.

"My name is Marguerite," the girl stammered as she put her hand in the lady's hand. The girl felt so proud that she was actually holding hands for that brief moment.

"Welcome to our village!" she said to Miriam.

"Thank you. You are so kind. You are really the first person I have met since we came here. I saw you one day when we were moving into our new home. You might like to see it when we finish putting everything together. It doesn't look very nice now. Perhaps you could invite your mother to come, too, so I could meet her."

"That would be so nice. I would like my mother to meet you. I know she would like you, and your family, too."

"I hope she does. I look forward to meeting her. Please tell her she would be most welcome at any time."

The girl ran home as fast as she could to tell her mother, who was at first displeased, thinking that her daughter had disebeyed her instructions. But when Marguerite told her mother that the lady had been standing right next to the shelf with the baking powder, she grinned. Marguerite also told her that the lady would like to meet her and that she was welcome to visit anytime, and that made her mother feel special.

Marguerite did follow her mother's instructions and did not go near those people again, though she could not help but see Joshua when he was playing with his new friends or going on errands for his parents. She just said hello to him and went about her business, though when he smiled at her when he said hello, she wanted so much to talk with him. However, she was obedient and did as her mother instructed.

One day, however, on her way to the playground, she saw him walking down the street. He must have just come from the lumberyard. He was carrying some big boards over his shoulder. One started to slip and then fell to the ground. He dropped the others and put his hands on his hips as if he was upset. Marguerite could not help herself. She ran over to help him. She could tell he was annoyed with himself for dropping the boards.

"It's not that it's too heavy," he said, "it's just that when one slips, they all slide off."

"Let me help you," Marguerite said. "I can carry one. I'd be glad to help you."

He looked at her, smiled, and then said, "Okay, thank you."

They both walked down the street and around the corner to his house. He seemed a little embarrassed that a girl was helping him, especially when a couple of her friends passed and giggled at them. Marguerite didn't mind, but she guessed a boy would be embarrassed that a girl had to help him, though it didn't *really* seem to bother him.

When they reached his house, Joshua's father was working on the front of it. He was building a porch. The old one had fallen apart. When he heard the two children talking, he turned and called to his son, "Joshua, you're back already. Good. You're just in time. I can use those pieces right here. Who's your new friend who's helping you?"

"Her name is Marguerite. The wood wasn't that heavy, Abba, but it kept slipping, so Marguerite offered to help me. It was very kind of her. I'd like to get her a glass of water and a piece of homemade bread that mother just baked. Is that all right, Abba?"

"Of course, Son. We should always be grateful when someone does us a kindness, but ask your mother first."

Standing near the porch waiting, the girl was wondering how Joshua knew her name since she had never talked to him, and was sure no one could have told him.

While she was lost in her thoughts, Joshua's father turned toward her and introduced himself. "My name is Joseph, Marguerite. Thank you for helping my son. He is such a good boy, and a big help to me. I get tired easily and he seems to sense it, so he always insists on helping me."

"He seems so different from the other boys in the village. He is very kind and gentle."

"He is that, all right. But he can be full of mischief some-times. He likes to play tricks, but nothing mean; just to make good fun."

"You said your name is Joseph. But Joshua calls you 'Abba.' "

Joseph laughed out loud. " 'Abba' means 'Daddy' in our language."

"Oh," the girl remarked.

At that point Joshua came out with a glass of water and a big slice of hot homemade bread. His mother came out with him.

"Marguerite, what a nice surprise to see you again! Thank you for helping my son carry that big load of wood."

"I was glad to help him, Miriam. The wood was awkward and kept slipping, so I knew he needed help. This homemade bread is delicious. Thank you both very much. I wish we had homemade bread at home. We buy ours at the store, but it's not as good as homemade."

Miriam smiled. "Thank you, Marguerite. I am glad you like it."

"I have to go home now. Good-bye. You are all such nice people," Marguerite said as she gave the empty glass back to Joshua, then half-walked and half-skipped down the street. Marguerite lived with her parents, Bill and Vivian McCabe, on Turtle Street.

"Joshua, would you bring the boards over here, so we can finish patching up this section. All we will have to do then is replace boards on the porch and paint everything, and the porch will look just like new."

"I like the way you work, Father. You make it look so easy."

"Son, when you know what you are doing, it is easy. That is why it is so important to learn everything you can when you are young, so you will have all the knowledge and experience you need to work efficiently later on. It is also important to plan everything thoroughly before you do something, so you don't make a lot of costly mistakes."

"I learn just from watching you, Father. I like working with you. You're also my best friend, so it's fun."

"Thank you, Son. That means a lot to me," Joseph replied as he put his hand on his son's head and smiled at him with a tear in his eye.

As Joshua looked up at his father, Joseph could see that his son's thoughts were in another time and another place.

He had seen that look in his son's eyes many times before, and though he said nothing, he wondered what was behind those thoughtful brown eyes, eyes that could see far beyond what was present.

The two worked hard on the house. As the family had little money, Joseph visited the Shadybrook lumber company one day and asked if they needed any help.

"You don't have to pay me a lot, just enough to buy some lumber and materials I need to work on my house."

It was a lucky day. Two men did not show up for work and the manager needed help. However, he insisted on paying Joseph well for his work, and said he could buy what he needed at an employee's discount. Joseph was thrilled and worked hard all day. At the end of the day, one of the workers drove him home in his truck, with all of Joseph's wood and materials. Joseph's pride shone through his happy smile, which made Miriam so proud. The man helped unload the truck. When they finished, Joseph invited him inside, but he had to get home for his own supper, which he knew his wife had all ready for him.

"HEY, KID," A BOY YELLED ACROSS THE STREET TO Joshua, who was helping his father. "Do you want to play baseball? We're a man short, so you're welcome to play with us."

"Go ahead, Son," Joseph said to him. "You've been working hard with me every day. You need to play. It's important."

"But, Father, who will help you?"

"Joshua, I have worked by myself all my life, so even though it's a lot easier when you help me, I'll manage until you get back. So, you go and play now, and have a good time."

Joshua was thrilled. He had played baseball a few times before and had had a lot of fun. And he was good at it besides. He was thrilled that the boy had asked him.

"My name's Jimmy. What's your name?" the boy asked.

"Joshua."

"You just moved here, didn't you? Where did you live before?"

"In different places. Washington, D.C., was the last place."

"You and your father are doing a real good job on your house. It used to be a mess before you came."

"Thank you. My father is a real carpenter. He's an expert, and I like helping him. He makes everything look easy, even hard jobs."

When the boys arrived at the field, the others were waiting. The sides had already been chosen, so the oldest boy told Joshua what team he was on, and what position he would play.

"Right field. Is that okay, kid?" the older boy asked.

"Yes, whatever you say. I'm just glad you invited me to play."

Before long the boys were well into the game. With all the noise they were making when someone got a hit, a crowd of young people began to gather. When it was Joshua's turn at bat, he got two strikes and two balls before he finally connected and hit a single out into left field. The next batter hit a double into right field and Joshua ran all the way home, giving his team its first run.

"Who's that kid?" one of the fans asked. "I never saw him before. He's fast. Did you see the way he ran around those bases?"

"He's the new kid who lives in that old broken-down shack on 'Mud Puddle Road.' "

That's the nickname the villagers had given to the street where Joshua lived. It had been practically abandoned by the village work crew, since no one of any importance lived there.

"That's no broken-down shack anymore," a girl commented. "Have you seen it lately? It's beautiful what the new family did to it. They must be artists or something. The boy is a nice kid. One of my friends knows him. He spends most of his time helping his father."

The next boy at bat hit into a double play and that ended the inning. By the end of the game, the score was three to two. Joshua's team lost, but they had fun. Afterward, they went down to the store to get cold drinks. As Joshua had no money, he just thanked the boys for inviting him to play and went home.

"Joshua, you can play with us anytime. You're good," George McHenry, a newfound friend, called to him.

"Thanks, George, I liked playing. It's fun."

Joshua found his father still working hard. The outside was finished. A second coat of paint was all that was needed. Joseph had pretty well finished the bathroom in the modern style, a real luxury for this simple family.

"Abba, that looks beautiful! How did you learn to do all these modern things?"

"Joshua, I watched others building homes and I learn quickly, so it was not very difficult. In fact, I really enjoyed it. Well, Son, I'm all finished now for the day. Let me wash up, and you and I can take a walk while Mother is preparing supper. We can have a little talk."

"Good, Abba. Let me splash some cold water on my face. I am all sweaty from playing baseball. It will help me cool off."

"I hope you two aren't going to be gone long," Miriam called from the kitchen. "I'm almost ready for supper, so don't take too long. I have a nice surprise for you both."

Joshua liked these frequent walks with his father. They shared everything, and a beautiful bond had developed between them. They were not only father and son. They were each other's best friend.

"How did your game go, Joshua?"

"It was fun, Father. I got a hit, a single. The next boy hit a double, and I ran all the way home."

"Home?" Joseph said with great surprise in his voice. "When did you come home? I didn't see you come home until just a few minutes ago."

Joshua laughed. "Father, I don't mean 'home' to the house. That's what they say when someone scores a point in the game. When someone runs around the four bases, the last base is called 'home.' When you do that, you get what they call a 'run.' Our team lost. We had only two runs. The other team had three runs. But that's all right. We had a lot of fun."

"You have a good attitude, Joshua. Games should be fun. When people take them too seriously, they're no longer fun."

"The boys on the team are good boys. I think I would like some of them for friends. One of them is named George."

"Do you like this little town, Son?"

"Very much. It's not like the big cities, where there's no place to play except in the streets. I like it where there are trees and fields and little lakes. It's peaceful and I like to hear the birds singing, and watch all the funny little animals. My Father in heaven likes to have fun, too. You can tell by all the funny and playful things in nature."

"I am glad you find joy in everything around you. Don't ever lose that happy spirit."

"I do worry about you, though, Father. You seem to have a lot of things that you worry about. It makes me sad."

"I know, Son. I want everything to be nice for you and your mother. You and your mother are so special to me. I always worry that something might happen to you."

"Don't worry, Father. Nothing will happen that my Father in heaven doesn't allow. And we have our work to do, so you can always be sure he'll protect us until it's done. Then, when it's done, we go back home."

"Joshua, everything is so simple for you. That is a wonderful way to be."

"It's true, though. I'll pray that you won't worry anymore."

"Thank you, Joshua. I am so glad that we are such good friends. I think we had better start for home. Your mother will be waiting for us."

"Father, I have to tell you something. I wanted to tell you before, but I didn't know whether I should."

"What is that, Son?"

"It's about the man who owns our house. I don't have good feelings about that man. Please be careful, Father. I notice he did not give you any papers to sign. I know I'm only a child, but I think it might be good to have a piece of paper between you before you do any more work on the house. I don't think that man can be trusted."

Tears began to well up in Joseph's eyes.

"Joshua, I know you are only a young boy, but your insight into grown-ups surprises me. Did you always feel that way about that man?"

"Yes, Father. I listened to the two of you when you made the agreement. I was surprised that he showed no interest in writing it down on a piece of paper, like I saw other people do. I know you're trusting and innocent, but most people don't have your goodness. I'm afraid that he might tell us to leave when you finish fixing the house and it looks beautiful. I was watching a fox running across a field yesterday, and I started to think about that man. I think he's like a fox."

"I will think hard on that tonight, and pray about it. I am really not a businessman, Son. I am an artist, and I don't understand the ways of the world. I count on God to help me, and to protect us from harm."

Miriam was sitting on the front porch sewing when her two men came home.

"Just in time. Everything is ready. I have nice surprises for you both."

"Father and I had a nice talk, Mother; you know, things that men talk about."

Mary looked at Joseph and they both smiled.

"Yes, we did have some men talk," Joseph responded. "Joshua has become quite a young man."

As soon as they went inside, Joseph clapped his hands and rubbed them together. "Miriam, you cooked my favorite supper, rice fried with chicken in orange and raisin sauce. We haven't had that in so long."

"And my favorite dessert: apples, raisins, and figs. I can smell them cooking," Joshua added excitedly. "Mother, you are too good to us, with all your other work."

"I really have a selfish motive when I do things to make you happy. It gives me such joy to see my two men so excited."

"Well, let's not just stand here making noise. Joshua, wash your hands and let's sit down and eat," Joseph said as he reached over and kissed his wife on the cheek. "Thank you, dear. I know it is a hot day to be cooking."

As they sat down and quietly expressed their thanks, Joseph poured water from a ceramic pitcher into everyone's glass. Their meals were such joyful times. Tired from their hard work each day, they looked forward to the evening meal, and their few minutes together. For them, simple as it was, it was more fun than rich people have dining at a five-star restaurant. Even though there was not a lot of food served, sharing with one another their day's experiences and thoughts stretched the meal out for over an hour.

While they were eating their chicken and rice, Joseph took a sip of water and looked shocked. "Miriam, I thought you put water in that pitcher."

"I did, dear."

"Taste it. That's not water. It's wine."

Miriam tasted a sip from her glass. "But, Joseph. It is water," she told him.

"Joshua, taste yours! What's in your glass?"

Joshua tasted his and quickly replied with a perfectly straight face, "Father, it's water."

Joseph's quizzical look showed he was still not convinced.

"Joseph, you must have had some wine in your glass before you poured water in it."

"Well, I have to admit, it's good wine so I'm not complaining about it. I was just surprised. Funny things happen around here sometimes. Besides, dear, this meal is so good. Thank you for being so good to us," Joseph said as he smacked his lips in approval.

"How about you, Joshua? Do you like yours?"

"I always like your cooking, Mother, but I can't wait for the dessert. That's my favorite."

Miriam's whole life centered on her two men. She knew Joseph worked hard to make life as comfortable as possible for their little family, and though at times life was difficult, she tried in little ways to brighten the atmosphere by such simple things as baking a favorite cake or preparing a special meal. The love they showed for each other made up for disappointing happenings or hurtful actions of unkind neighbors, like the time when someone scrawled a nasty note telling them their nice little village didn't need poor scum like them living in their neighborhood, and insisting that they leave and go somewhere else, like out in the woods where they wouldn't be lowering the property values of their neighbors.

Incidents like this were rare, but when they happened, they hurt. Joseph particularly felt bad because it was a reflection on himself and his ability to provide a well-to-do lifestyle for his family. At times like that, Joshua felt his father's unspoken pain and would walk over to him and, putting his hand on Joseph's shoulder, say with deep conviction, "Abba, the value of a person is not in how many worldly goods he possesses or his position in the community, but in the nobility of his soul. You tower above everyone in Shadybrook by the beauty of what my Father in heaven sees in your heart. Don't feel bad because we have little in worldly possessions. They are nothing compared to what we have in each other. There isn't a father in the world who could compare to you. People in this village may look like they have a lot to recommend them, but when my Father in heaven looks at them, he sees so many empty shells."

Whenever Joshua would speak like this, Joseph would turn his head and, with a tear in his eye, look straight at his son and tell him, "Joshua, I don't know where your wisdom comes from, but you have the rare gift to see through people's souls and take away their pain. You are so right, Son. We have a rare and precious treasure in each other. And your mother and I are so fortunate to have you for a son."

I T WAS OVER SIX WEEKS SINCE JOSHUA'S FAMILY moved into what was to be their home. It did not take long before townsfolk realized that Joshua's father was a master carpenter to have transformed the dilapidated building into a real modern home. Even the landscaping was done with good taste, though it was done with shrubs and wildflowers that Joshua and his father had dug up in the woods and transplanted around their house.

Joshua wasn't aware that there were so many beautiful flowers and shrubs growing wild in the woods and in little out-of-the-way places. Some of the plants around their house were just beginning to bloom, and they looked so pretty. Joshua's mother watered them all every evening. For someone passing the house each day, the progress was dramatic, even from what it had been only the day before. It was fast becoming one of the prettiest houses in the village, so different from what it had been for as long as anyone could remember.

As the lazy days of summer moved slowly, Joshua spent much of his time working with his father and going on occasional errands for his mother or to the supply store for materials. Whenever he met his friends on the street, he was always friendly and called each of them by name, which made them feel special, but he couldn't spend much time with them.

Before long, when much of the outside work on the house was well along, Joseph insisted that Joshua spend more time playing baseball with his friends. Sometimes Marguerite would go with her girlfriends and watch the boys play. She would always applaud for Joshua's team. Her friends noticed it and teased her about it. Even some of them applauded for his side. He was a good player, and a lot better than the first time he played. Whenever he hit the ball, it would really go far. Most of the boys liked Joshua because he was fun, and was playful. There was one boy, however, who didn't like Joshua. Everyone knew it would be just a matter of time before there would be trouble because this boy was a bully, and would start fights with younger boys. Joshua was always nice to the boy, but even when he was nice, the fellow seemed to resent it.

One day it happened. Joshua had just come back from a baseball game and was walking through the village. A gang was gathering in the park. Two boys were fighting. Well, they were not actually fighting; the kid who hated Joshua was pushing a boy considerably smaller than himself, trying to goad him into a fight. The boy was so scared, all he wanted to do was run, but there was no way to escape. The other kids kept taunting him. Marguerite and her friends were watching from a distance and felt bad for the little fellow. He was no match for the bully. The kid wanted to cry, but was brave enough to hold back the tears. There was nothing the girls could do.

Joshua approached the crowd and realized what was happening. He worked his way into the circle and, looking at the bully, called his name.

"Hey, MacIntosh! Do you always pick on little kids? I've seen bullies like you before, and you're all the same. You're cowards. You think it will make you feel good if you beat up a little kid."

This was just the chance the bully was waiting for. Beet-red with rage at being humiliated, he forgot the boy and turned toward Joshua as if to take him on. Joshua was also smaller than MacIntosh.

"Okay, smart guy, big hero. You fight me, then," he said to Joshua.

"What does fighting prove, even if you win? And if I win, it still proves nothing. I'll ask you just one question. Answer the question and then I'll tell you whether I'll fight you or not. Would you tell all of us what happened last night?"

The fellow turned from beet-red to ashen, as if all his blood was suddenly drained from him. He said nothing, but dropped his fists and walked out of the circle and down the street. The crowd broke up and drifted off. Jimmy, the little boy whom Joshua had protected, came over to Joshua and stammered a timid thank you.

"No need to thank me, Jimmy. You have to learn not to be afraid. Fear can paralyze you and prevent you from doing many things you would like to do." Jimmy held his hand out to Joshua. They shook, and Jimmy started on his way home. Joshua continued on his way. He knew he would be late helping his father.

As he walked down the street, the girls approached him and asked him what had happened the night before. Joshua merely laughed and said that that was MacIntosh's secret. The girls were not to be put off, however, and were determined to find out what had happened. Girls seem to have a way of finding out things, and sure enough, by that night they all knew just what had taken place the night before.

A group of girls had come upon the bully picking on a girl, and he was pushing her around while she kept crying. The other girls grabbed hold of the bully and knocked him down, then took off his shoes and socks and ran off with them. The MacIntosh boy had to walk down the street to his house in his bare feet, totally humiliated.

ALL THE WORK JOSEPH PUT INTO THE HOUSE was beginning to show what an expert craftsman he was. It did not take long for his reputation to spread through the village. One day a frail elderly lady walked down the lane and asked Joseph, who was working on the house, if he could fix some things around her place. Joseph responded with a smile and told her he would be happy to help her. She told him her address and they made arrangements for a time when Joseph could stop over to her house and see what had to be done.

Even though Joshua was a help to his father, Joseph continually encouraged the boy to spend more time with his friends. The baseball season was well on its way, and as the weather was warmer, the village swimming pool was about to open. That meant swim teams would be set and competitions would begin soon. Joshua's friends tried to interest him in joining, but he always declined. One day after a baseball game, Marguerite and her friends approached him and asked him point-blank why he kept saying no.

"Because I have so many other things I have to do."

"But your father has most of the outside of the house finished, so he doesn't need your help as much now as he did. So, why don't you sign up for one of the swim teams?"

Joshua failed to give the girls a straight answer, and they finally gave up. Marguerite suspected the real reason why he always declined. Shadybrook village charged fees to use the pool, and Joshua's family was poor. Joshua probably did not want to ask his parents for money they did not have, so it was easier for him to say no. So she and her friends went to the lady in charge of the pool and told her the story, and how the kids would love to have Joshua on one of the swim teams because he was a real good athlete. And as teenagers do not usually give up if they really want something, the girls kept trying to persuade the director, Betty Cashin. Eventually she gave in. The agreement was that if Joshua was willing to help her with the work that had to be done around the pool and the grounds, she would let him use the pool and be part of the competition.

"But don't ask me for any more exceptions," Betty told the girls, "because I cannot do this for everybody. But I do need one boy to help around here, and only one, and your friend is it."

"Thanks, Betty. You won't regret it. Joshua is real special. You'll see."

"I hope so."

Marguerite could not wait to tell Joshua. She met him as he was on his way back from the building supply store.

"Joshua, the lady in charge of the village swimming pool asked if I knew a boy who would be willing to help her with the work that needed to be done around the pool and the grounds. I told her that I knew someone who would be excellent at that and told her about you. She would like to see you."

"Oh, that was thoughtful of you, Marguerite. I don't know if I would be able to do that. I do help my father, and baseball takes time, too."

"But, Joshua, don't say no right out. Think about it. And if you do take the job, you'll be able to be on the swim team and use the pool for practice and everything."

Joshua then realized what the real story was. He smiled. "Do they really want me to be on the swim team?"

"Of course they do. You have become part of everything they do now, and they know you'll be good on the swim team, too. So, don't say no before you think about it."

"I'll think about it."

"At least go and talk to Miss Cashin at the pool. She'll be expecting you. She desperately needs someone to help her."

"Okay, I'll do that, first thing tomorrow morning."

"Promise?"

"I promise," Joshua said with a quiet laugh, and continued on his way home.

Then he turned and called back, "Thank you, Marguerite. You're a good friend."

The next morning, first thing, Joshua went to see Miss Cashin.

"Miss Cashin, I'm Joshua. Marguerite told me you would like to see me."

"Yes, Joshua. Thank you for coming. I do need someone here to help me with some of the work that has to be done around here. It's not hard work, but I can't do it all by myself."

"I can do hard work, too, Miss Cashin. I'm used to it. I help my father, who is a master craftsman."

"I'm sure you can, Joshua, but we'll see. In the meantime, I'll show you the kind of work that needs to be done. If you're willing to help me, you can start whenever you like. I can't afford to pay salaries, but I can let you use the pool and be part of the swim teams. The work will take only an hour or two each day."

As the woman showed Joshua what had to be done, he realized it was not a big job, and it was something he could fit into his schedule, so as she finished showing him around, he told her he would be willing to take the job.

"You can start tomorrow if you like, Joshua. Can you work from ten in the morning till noon? If you can, that would be perfect."

"That would work out. I help my father before that time and I could be here by ten o'clock."

The two shook hands on that and Joshua walked off happy, knowing that he could now be on one of the swim teams. He couldn't wait to go home and tell his mother he had a real job, and that even though it did not pay anything, he would be allowed to use the village pool and be on one of the swim teams.

"Son, I am so proud of you," she said to him as he told her about his interview. "You are growing up to be quite the young man. I know you will do a good job."

"I will. I want you and Father to be proud of me."

"I am already proud of you, Joshua," his father said as he came in through the back door.

"Joshua, can you help me make a mailbox for out front?"

"A mailbox. That will be fun. Do you want me to draw a nice one, or is it going to be just an ordinary mailbox like everybody has?"

"Well, if you can draw one, if it's practical, we can make it. But, I will need it soon as I would like to put it up today."

"Okay, Abba, I'll do it right now, then I'll help you make it."

"Good."

The boy went to it immediately, spreading the paper out on the kitchen table and asking his mother if she had any ideas.

"I don't know anything about things like that. You just use your imagination."

It did not take long. "Mother, I have a good idea already. It will be like an old-fashioned fishing boat, the same size as other mailboxes, but the front will open down to put the mail in and take it out. There will be a sail on the top, which can be put up if there's mail for the mailman to take, or stay down if there isn't any."

When he finished, he ran out to show his father, who was painting the front porch. His father looked at the drawing and with a broad grin asked, "Joshua, what is it with you and those fishing boats?"

"Why, Abba, don't you like it?"

"It's clever, but you seem fascinated with those old fishing boats."

"I guess they seem to bring back a lot of memories, nice memories, and I like thinking about that."

"Okay. It seems the right size and it looks practical enough. Let's see if we can put it together."

It took the rest of the morning, but they finally finished it just in time for lunch. It did take work because there was a lot of carving and shaping that had to be done. But the finished product was elegant. They were both proud of it, and they couldn't wait to show Miriam. When she saw it, she thought it was beautiful.

It seemed each day was a new adventure for the family. Nothing dramatic or sensational like in some people's lives, but simple happenings and new surprises. Joshua, in his simplicity, enjoyed every new thing that happened. Every day he was like a child waking up on Christmas morning for the first time. There are some rare people like that, for whom even the simplest of pleasures are cause for sheer delight. It is always a joy to be in the presence of such people. For those of us who are not like that, just to see their joy makes us realize how much in life we miss by being too sophisticated or too detached from the simple things in life. They make life exciting and their joy is infectious.

Even though Joshua and his family seemed so simple and lighthearted, it was not always true. No sooner had Joseph and Joshua finished all the renovations on the house, and beautified the grounds, and planted a garden, than the owner, Mr. Jenkins, came to visit Joseph and told him that he and his family had to move. He had a buyer for the house. What had been pressing on Joshua's heart for so long had finally come to pass. Miriam was devastated, more out of concern for Joseph and all the hard work he and Joshua had put into making the house look so beautiful.

"But we had an agreement," Joseph said to the man.

With a cynical laugh, Jenkins retorted, "Agreements are made to be broken."

While Joseph was a prudent man, and brave enough, he was not a fighter. But Joshua was, and when he heard what the man was saying to his father, his anger flared as he walked in on the two of them. The man could see from the anger flashing in the boy's eyes that this kid was going to be trouble. What was even more unsettling to Jenkins was the boy's discipline over his anger.

"I heard you make that agreement with my father, and if you intend to go on with this, it will not go well for you. I will testify on my father's behalf, and the judge will listen to me even though I am only a boy. And because of how the people in town feel about you, they will be in court to support us. The people know you from way back. They know you are a man filled with greed and love of money. You care for nothing and no one, and you have hurt many innocent people."

"You little brat! You had better leave this house by the end of the week or I'll have you thrown out. You got that straight?"

"If my father agrees, we'll see you in court first. People have to learn to stand up to mean people like you. You are an evil man."

"My son is right. I do not intend to take this without a fight. We entered into our contract with you in good faith, and we intend to pursue our just cause. The next move is yours, because we are not leaving here."

Jenkins did not expect this from a family he considered just simple, ignorant people. Although he still intended to take over his house, it was not going to be simple. He would have to follow legal procedures to evict the family. Though Joseph was nervous because he did not like all this fuss, Joshua was different. He was determined that his father and mother were not going to be treated so shabbily and lose their place to live, and his little mind was working like a high-speed computer wondering what to do next.

As Jenkins left in a huff, it was with the threat, "You'll regret what just happened here, and what you've said. Mark my words! You'll pay for this."

Joseph had never liked conflict. He had always tried to avoid it to save his family from the anxiety and misery it would inevitably cause. This situation was different, however, and he knew he had to take a firm stand, though he did not feel at all comfortable with Joshua interfering the way he had. It was embarrassing. He knew Joshua was right, but if it was just between the landlord and himself, he might have been able to talk him into being more reasonable.

Joseph said nothing to Joshua, but Joshua knew he was annoyed. He also knew that there was nothing his father could have said or done that would have changed the man's mind. Joshua knew he and his father were in the better position if the matter went to court, which would happen the very next week, when the next court session was scheduled. By that time the judge would have become familiar with the case. Since everyone knew everybody else in town, hearsay passing through the neighborhood would have filtered back to the judge and given him a good insight into what he was dealing with. All he needed was testimony from Mr. Jenkins and Joseph, and possibly from Joshua if his testimony could be admissible because of his age.

On the night of the court session, the small room was packed. Neighbors who had grown to love Joseph and Miriam and Joshua packed the courtroom to show their support, and also to show how they felt about Mr. Jenkins, for whom they had nothing but disdain. This was not the first time he had done mean things to defenseless people.

The judge was a sharp lawyer, and after allowing each side to present its position, he asked only a few questions. The first was to Mr. Jenkins.

"Mr. Jenkins, you said you allowed the family to live in the house under discussion. Is that correct?"

"Yes, your honor."

"Since the house had been closed by the building inspector for the past three years, did you receive the necessary permits to work on the house, and a certificate of occupancy to allow the new family to live there?"

Mr. Jenkins stumbled over his answer, not knowing how

to reply. If he said no, the judge would find him in violation of the law. He finally responded, "Your honor, I did tell the family that after he repaired the house, I would allow him and his family to live there."

"And did they repair the house to the point where it was livable?"

"Well, yes, I suppose you could say that, your honor."

"I had the building inspector check the house before this meeting," the judge said. "The inspector reported that considerable work had been done on the house and the grounds as well. In fact, his report stated that the present condition of the house indicates the highest quality of workmanship. I am sure you are aware of that. But the inspector also reported that you never applied for permits to have work done on the house, nor did you apply for a certificate of occupancy. Is that true, Mr. Jenkins?"

"I suppose I would have to say yes, your honor. I have been very busy and must have overlooked some details."

"Details, Mr. Jenkins?"

"Important details, your honor. I did not mean to imply that the applications were not important, your honor."

"You are aware, Mr. Jenkins, that there are severe penalties for having overlooked those 'details,' as you call them. And I will direct the village officials to calculate what your financial responsibility is for not having honored those rules of the building code. They will be contacting you in the near future."

"Yes, your honor."

"Now, to come to the issue at hand. You have already admitted that you agreed to allow the family to live in the house on what is commonly called 'Mud Puddle Road' in return for their repairing and renovating it. My question now is: Is it true that after they finished all the renovations, you told them that they could not live there and that they would have to leave?"

"Well, yes, your honor. I felt it is my house, and I got a very generous offer for it, which I could not turn down."

"And in accepting this offer, you realized that you had broken the agreement you made with the family concerned, a valid and binding contract even though it was made only verbally?"

"I suppose I would have to agree with you, your honor."

"Mr. Jenkins, and Mr. Ben-Yacob [which was Joseph's family name], I am placing two alternatives before you. The first, Mr. Jenkins, is to honor your agreement that the Ben-Yacob family live in the house on the commonly called 'Mud Puddle Road' as long as they wish, since there were no restrictions in your agreement on the length of time they could live in that house if they renovated it.

"The second possibility is that the family will move from the house, in return for you compensating them for the total renovation of the house and grounds. This compensation must be based on the prevailing rates for an accomplished craftsman multiplied by the total hours spent on the planning and actual renovation of the building and grounds, plus the cost of materials for the work done. Added to this will be the cost of two years of rent in a house of comparable value, since they will be deprived of their free rent for whatever number of years they would have been living on Mud Puddle Road."

"But, your honor, the amount would be astronomical."

"That is my decision, Mr. Jenkins. The amount is comparable to the value of what that family has done for you, and the value of what you had promised them. If your house has value now, it is due to the expertise and hard work of Mr. Ben-Yacob. So, his compensation should recognize that."

"Your honor, you don't give me much choice," Mr. Jenkins responded.

His resentment at the decision was obvious, but he dared not express what he was really thinking. All he said was, "The family can live there as long as they keep it in good condition."

"Mr. Ben-Yacob, are you satisfied with Mr. Jenkins's decision, which will be accepted and enforced by this court?" the judge asked.

"Yes, your honor."

"This case is closed. Court is dismissed," concluded the judge, who stood up and walked back into his chambers to the loud applause of the whole crowd. Even the townspeople felt a sense of vindication at what they had put up with on the part of Mr. Jenkins's arrogance for so many years.

Since that night, Joseph and his family had become village heroes. There was not a soul in town who did not hear about what had transpired. It served to make everyone aware of the plight of the little family, and they expressed their thoughtfulness in many small ways for Joseph's courage in bringing the case to court. It was also a recognition that people looked upon the family as poor, which embarrassed Joshua, who, as a proud young boy, did not want people to think that his family was needy when he knew that they did not really need anything more than the simple things they already had, especially their love for one another, which for him was real wealth.

NOW THAT THEY HAD THE LEGAL RIGHT TO LIVE in the house, the family felt more at peace. It is one thing to be homeless in a land where the climate is warm, but in a place where the cold can be brutal, it is not even thinkable. So, as detached as the family was from unnecessary material things, concern about having a place to live was understandable. Even Joshua felt more comfortable. In fact, as young as he was, he was the first to show concern over the possibility that, knowing what the landlord was like, they might not have a place to live.

That weekend, on Saturday morning, the family took a bus to the city to attend religious services. On Sunday morning they attended church in the village, where they could receive Communion.

When the new week started, Joseph went to work at the lumber mill, where his work was becoming more and more permanent. The owner appreciated his expertise and his congenial personality. Joseph worked well and felt comfortable following instructions, which the owner also appreciated. Not every employee can take instructions graciously without expressing a better way of doing something. The owner felt doubly happy with Joseph.

The work that remained to be done on the house was minimal, and it was mostly inside work like painting Joshua's room and finishing the upstairs bathroom. The nicest room in the house was the one Joseph had asked Miriam to pick out for her workroom. She loved to spend time making clothes for her family, her own included. That room was the first one to be finished, and Mariam was happy as a queen, being able to start work on her many projects, one of the first of which was making clothes for a baby who had just been born into a poor family that lived not far away. Joshua had become aware of them when he heard his friends talking about them at the playground one day. They were talking about the family being poor, and the boy had to help at home because they just had another baby.

After the game, Joshua went home and told his mother about the family, dropping a hint that they probably needed help. His mother smiled at his thoughtfulness and decided to make some clothes and a blanket for the baby.

"I guess I am bringing him up right," she thought, as if to reassure herself.

When it came to doing nice things like this for people, Joshua and his mother collaborated. Joshua picked up information outside and then scouted around to see what was needed. He would tell his mother and she did the rest, with his help. Sometimes they needed to ask for Joseph's help if what he could do was needed. Whatever they did was done with such delicacy as to make the people think they were honoring them by accepting their simple gifts.

As Joseph did not need Joshua's help as much as before,

Joshua was spending more time with his friends. He liked people, so he was happiest when he was with his playmates, mostly the boys, but he also enjoyed the girls because they were more lighthearted and at times could be more fun.

One day a group of girls was standing around as the boys were practicing before a game. Marguerite was among them with a girlfriend who was a very good baseball player. Marguerite had told Joshua one day that this girl, Jane, was the best player on the girls' team, but that her dream was to play on the boys' team. Joshua smiled and just commented, "This is going to be interesting."

"Do you think they will let Jane play?" she asked Joshua.

"Well, I don't know, but if you think she's really good, we could try."

"She is really good. Would you like to see her play first? Then you can tell for yourself."

"Okay, that's a good idea."

The next day Joshua went to the girls' game and sat on the side with Marguerite to watch her friend. After only a few innings, Joshua was impressed.

"Marguerite, you're right. Jane is good. I'll talk to the boys and see what they say."

The boys were against it in the beginning, but when Joshua talked them into letting her try out so they could see for themselves, they agreed to go along, though they were not enthusiastic. As the team gathered in the early afternoon, Marguerite and Jane were standing on the side with their friends. The boys put together a choose-up game and included Jane, and they were dumbfounded to see how well she played. One of the boys commented, "She doesn't even throw funny or bat funny the way girls do. And she can run fast."

One boy commented, "She's even better than some of

us." She could certainly hit better than some of them and definitely run faster than most of them. They agreed to give her a try.

When the other teams heard about this, they were beside themselves. They immediately protested and said if the girl played, they would refuse to play against them. Joshua's friends did not want their little league to disband and were thinking of giving in. A big discussion ensued.

"Why give in to them?" Joshua spoke up.

Boys from other teams were gathering around, upset because a girl was playing.

"Why are you upset?" Joshua asked them. "Are you afraid you can't beat us if she plays?"

"That's not the reason," one of the older boys complained. "We just never had girls play. They play funny, and they run funny, and they throw the ball funny, and well, we just don't want girls playing."

"Well, why don't we at least give it a try?" Joshua said in an attempt to be democratic. "We can play one game, and after the game, if you find that she can't play as well as the boys, and if she plays funny, as you say, then we can decide what we want to do."

Reluctantly, they all agreed. Joshua knew they would be impressed. And they were, very impressed. Eventually the other teams let girls join, too. It even made the games more exciting, as the boys were just beginning to realize what girls were all about, and they were beginning to notice every now and then that one or another of them could actually be likable for other unusual reasons, reasons they had never even considered before.

"Good move, Joshua! Good move!" the boys would say to him whenever one of the girls did well. Joshua beamed with delight that they could all have such fun together.

Marguerite did not get on a team. She was a little too shy to step forward, but she still came to many of the games with some of her friends, just to watch. Everyone knew she liked Joshua and would become all excited when he got a hit, or even caught a fly ball. Her friends would laugh at her, but she would merely say, "I can't help it, I like him. I think he's cool. And besides, he's kind."

A crisis erupted when an outside team was visiting Shadybrook. The outsiders had heard that there were girls on village teams, but thought it was just a rumor. When they found that it was true, they insisted that the girls be removed from the team before they would play them.

To give the village team credit, they refused to leave the girls out. "Are you afraid the girls might beat you?" one of the boys asked the captain of the visiting team.

When he did not answer, the boy pursued the issue. "Well, if you're not afraid of losing, why not play? Who knows, you might even end up with girls on your team. It makes the games a lot more exciting."

The visitors left the village without the issue being resolved. However, when the playoffs took place, the outside team, the Bears, did not want to jeopardize their chance to win by refusing to play, as they had a good chance to win.

The flap over girls joining the teams did not last long. The outside teams could not afford to continue the issue for fear of giving up their chance to win the playoffs. When Joshua's team had seen that not all girls pitched funny, or ran funny, and that some of them were faster and sharper than some of the boys, they were glad they had decided to include them on the team.

The summer was drawing to a close, and it was almost time for the playoffs to see who had the best team. There were still three teams in close competition with one another:

the Bears, the Foxes, and the Coyotes. Joshua's team was the Foxes. The Bears had won most of their games, and the Coyotes were not far behind. The Foxes were two games behind the Coyotes.

When the time came for the playoffs, the Foxes and Coyotes played three games. The winner of those games would then play the Bears. Of the three games the Foxes won two. They now had to play the Bears, who everyone knew had a much better team. All the kids watching the games were surprised that the Foxes played well, though no one thought there was any hope they could beat the Bears.

The first game the Bears won easily. The second game the Foxes won because the Bears' pitcher walked three men when there was one man on. That gave the Foxes the run they needed to win.

The big day finally came. Kids from all over the area came to the village to watch. Everyone thought it would be a massacre. The Bears were up first. The first batter got a single, but a double play canceled out that hit. The third batter hit another single, and the fourth struck out.

Now it was the Foxes' turn. John MacIntosh was the first up. He hit a single to left field. The next batter was, of all people, John's newfound friend, Jimmy Cronin. Jimmy really wanted to do well so others would begin to like him. He was trying so hard to make friends. The first two pitches were balls. On the third pitch Jimmy hit a foul ball. The fourth pitch was a strike. The next pitch was a perfect pitch, right down the middle. Jimmy swung, and the ball flew out into right center field. It was the first good hit for Jimmy in weeks. He got a double while John MacIntosh scored the first run. The fans went wild. No one expected anything like that to happen. From second base Jimmy looked over at Joshua. Joshua signaled his approval with a raised thumb.

Jimmy beamed. The next two batters grounded out, and the third hit a pop fly that ended the inning.

The Foxes held the lead for three innings. Everyone was amazed. But then the Bears started scoring. They got two runs in the fourth inning and another one in the fifth. The score was now 3–1. The Foxes started to lose confidence. Their captain tried to cheer them up, but it didn't help. In the bottom of the fifth, the Foxes' first batter got a single, and at that point Joshua made an observation. He had noticed that if a batter kept shifting his feet before the ball was pitched, it made the Bears pitcher nervous and he lost focus. He suggested that each batter keep shifting his feet just before the pitch. Everyone thought it was funny, but no one believed it.

However, Jane heard what Joshua said, and she was up at bat. Just before the pitch she did as Joshua suggested, and the way she did it was really funny. Everyone could tell it rattled the pitcher. His first two pitches were wild. The next pitch almost hit Jane. Realizing he was losing control, he tried to calm down. But it did not help. He made the mistake of pitching a slow ball and it was just what Jane needed. She slammed it way out into deep right center field, and because she was so fast she got an inside-the-park home run. The score was now even, 3–3. In the top of the sixth inning the Bears got another run and were now ahead 4–3.

Now it was the bottom of the sixth, the Foxes' last chance. The first batter did what Joshua had suggested and kept shuffling his feet. The pitcher was openly annoyed, but the first pitch was a strike. The next two were balls, and the third one hit the batter. With one man on, it was now Joshua's turn to bat. He had gotten only one hit in the whole game. He now had a chance to try his strategy.

By this time the pitcher knew the foot-shuffling was intentional, and he lost his cool. The coach went out to the mound and tried to calm him down. The first pitch was a strike. Joshua stayed calm, and as the next pitch came right down the middle, Joshua prepared himself and swung. The ball went clear out into deep left center field, too far for the fielder to throw it all the way back to the infield. It reached the shortstop on a bounce. By that time, one runner had reached home, tying the score at 4–4, with Joshua at second.

The next batter hit a single and Joshua scored. The Foxes won! All their fans kept cheering and could not contain their excitement.

Shadybrook's mayor had planned a party for all the village teams, with prizes for the winners and outstanding players. The Bears left and the Foxes went to their homes to rest and shower and dress for the party. At seven o'clock they all assembled at the village hall. The party was fun. Parents and the small group of loyal fans who had hung in there all during the season were also invited.

It was a perfect finish for a perfect summer. When awards were given out, Joshua got the award for being the most improved player of the season. He accepted it with good humor. His mother and Joseph were proud of their son. He was happy he had so many friends.

Marguerite's mother arrived toward the end of the party to make sure her daughter got home safe. Joshua's parents were just coming out of the hall and they all met at the entrance.

"Mother," Marguerite said. "You're finally going to meet Joshua and his parents."

"Mother, this is Miriam, and this is Joseph, and this is Joshua," she said excitedly.

Her mother was taken aback. She expected to see poor people in shabby clothes, but they did not at all look poor, and she was impressed with the sense of dignity they all possessed, even their son, Joshua. But their dignity was not at all stuffy or reserved. They broke out into a warm greeting as they were introduced, and Miriam reached out to hug the woman she had wanted to meet for so long.

"My name is Vivian. In her excitement, my daughter forgot to tell you. I am so happy to have finally met you all. Marguerite has been telling me what a beautiful family you are. I'm sorry I haven't had a chance to meet you sooner. I hope we can get together sometime."

"I would like that very much," Miriam said, and Joseph finally added, "You are most welcome to our home anytime. And you can bring Marguerite with you, too. She is a delightful young lady."

Marguerite beamed.

6

As summer was coming to a close, Shady-brook was ending its outdoor recreational programs. A final swimming competition was the last item on the schedule. There were four teams. Joshua was a better baseball player than a swimmer, but they all wanted him to be on one of the teams.

One day he had an unsettling experience. Rather than go to the village pool to practice, because he felt conscious that he really could not afford to pay his way, he sometimes went out to the pond he found on the back road. On this particular day it was hot and muggy. It was a good day to practice and also just to take a swim in the cool water.

As he stripped and walked toward the edge of the pond and started to wade in the shallow water, he noticed his feet were not sinking, and he began walking on top of the water. Frightened, he put his clothes back on and ran home as fast as he could to tell his mother what had happened. Maybe she would understand.

When he came running into the house sweating and totally out of breath, his mother panicked.

"Joshua, what happened? You look so frightened. Are you all right? What happened, Son?"

"Mother, I don't know how to explain this to you. I'm so frightened."

"What happened?"

"Well, I was walking down the back road. It was so hot and humid, I decided to take a swim in the pond down there. When I waded into the water, I didn't sink. After taking a few steps I was still walking on top of the water, and I didn't sink. After taking a few more steps I was still walking on top of the water. I got so frightened. What's wrong with me, Mother? Am I odd? Am I a freak? I want to be like everybody else, and I keep noticing that I'm different, and in other ways, too."

Joshua thought for a moment, then said, "Like a while back. Remember when you put water in the pitcher before supper, and father poured some in all our glasses. You and I had water in ours, but father had wine in his."

"What do you mean, Son?"

"I knew father was tired from working so hard, and I thought he should have a glass of wine to relax him and help him rest, so I thought about that and then father complained that he had wine in his glass. I didn't want to say anything. But, things like that can happen when I wish them to happen. I also know what things happen in people's lives, especially when bad things happen to good people, and when they feel pain, I feel it, too. I just know something must be wrong with me, Mother."

"Son, sit down at the table with me and I will explain some things to you that are very important, things you should know. Here, drink this glass of orange juice, and drink it slowly. Just don't swallow it all at once."

Miriam began to explain things to her son that she had always wanted to share with him, but she never knew when was the right time. Now, it was clearly the right time.

"Son, many years ago, before you were born, an angel appeared to me and told me I was going to have a child, and that that child would be a very special child, and very close to God. The angel told me that that child should be named Joshua. You are that child. When we presented you to God, the priest Simeon recognized you as the anointed of God and was all excited to meet you before he died, as God promised him. He predicted that God had special work for you to do, and that your life would not be easy."

"Mother, why have you never told me these things before?"

"I wanted to, Son, but it never seemed the proper time. I guess now is the proper time."

"But, why do I have to have all these things that make me so different from everybody else? It makes me feel very uncomfortable with myself."

"Son, I don't know how to explain all those things to you. All I can understand is that you are very close to God. Even if I don't fully understand what that means. You are just going to have to gradually come to an understanding of that yourself. It is between you and God. I notice you keep calling God your 'Father in heaven.' It seems you already sense that you are God's son in a very special way.

"Your heavenly Father will have to help you to understand who you are. The unusual abilities you have are part of what your Father in heaven has given you. They are part of who you are. You are not a freak. You are very special to

God. You are a very blessed child. So, these abilities you have, keep them to yourself, and be grateful, and do not be afraid to use them for good.

"The time will come when those gifts will be very useful in helping others. And always remember that every child is different from every other child, and each has different gifts to do different kinds of work for God. You are not the only child who feels that he is different. Every young person has that feeling. No one wants to be different. Young people want more than anything to be just like everyone else. But, God did not make everyone just like everybody else. He made each one different for a reason, so that each one could be important and needed by others for things that others need."

"Mother, that helps a lot, but it doesn't answer all my questions. Maybe one day I'll be able to understand."

"In the meantime, Son, just enjoy the beauty of each day, and don't spend all your time being anxious about so many things. Your Father in heaven will take care of you. I am glad you feel comfortable enough to share everything with me."

"I am, too, Mother, because I know that Father would never understand."

Feeling more at peace, Joshua decided to go back down to the pond and take his swim. This time he was careful to see if he could just wade in like everybody else. He could. That made him feel much better. He tried a second time, this time deciding to try to walk on top of the water. He found that he could do that, too, if he decided.

"This is fun," he said to himself. Then he remembered what his mother had said to him, to keep all these things to himself. Then he went in and enjoyed swimming in the cool, clear water. He liked being alone. He felt at peace, and as he liked to live with his thoughts, he could do a lot of thinking when he was alone.

Sitting against a tree on the shore, he thought about what his mother had said, and he began to think about God. "Why did God make me different?"

In a few minutes he was sound asleep and dreaming of wandering through another world, a world that seemed so familiar to him, and so peaceful. Everyone seemed to know him and came over to welcome him. Some were human and some were different. Why did he feel so at home in this place? And the presence of God was so real. When he woke up he was happy and at peace.

From that time on, he often had similar experiences of that same familiar place, and each time felt a new intimacy with God. It was as if he had lived in that place a long time ago, and that his memory of that time was just beginning to come alive. On his walk back home, he saw the fox slinking across the field again, every now and then looking back over his shoulder as if expecting someone or something to come up behind it.

Back home, his mother noticed his changed mood. "You seem a lot more relaxed, Joshua."

"I feel much better. Thank you for helping me. I found that I can wade in the water, or, if I choose, I can also walk on the water. That's a nice feeling, but I will keep it to myself," Joshua said to her as he walked over and kissed her on the cheek.

"Where's Father?"

"I think he is out in the back yard taking a rest. There's a nice breeze out there. I think he may have dozed off. He works so hard."

Joshua looked out the kitchen window. Joseph was lying

comfortably in a lounge chair under the cherry tree, sound asleep.

"Mother, is Father okay?"

"Joshua, there you go worrying again. Why do you worry so much?"

"I worry because I understand a lot of things about people I love. I see things that sometimes I wish I did not see, not just about Father, but about my friends, and even about people who are strangers. I try not to worry, but it is very difficult. I know sometimes things that are going to happen, and it is hard not to worry. I don't like being anxious.

"I have to learn to discipline my feelings and realize that this is my Father in heaven's business, and everything has a reason. Sometimes I feel that there is a part of me that is human and a part of me that is more than human and very close to my Father in heaven. It is that part of me that sees things that haven't even happened yet, good things as well as bad things."

Miriam said nothing, but turned away and cried silently as she remembered that saintly old priest, Simeon, who had long ago said to her that "this boy will be a sign of contradiction, and is destined for the rise and fall of many, and that your own soul a sword shall pierce that the thoughts of many would be revealed." Tears then flowed freely down her cheeks as she walked over to her son and held him close to her. They hugged each other, and in that tender embrace they both understood. No words were needed.

"Well, Son, enough of this. Let's get back down to earth. I need you to go to the store and get me a half dozen ears of corn. Your father loves fresh corn, that Silver Queen variety. You had better get some real butter. He doesn't like that make-believe butter. Here's the money, and if you meet your friends, tell them you have to get home. I know you like to talk."

"I'll be back in a few minutes, Mother."

Sure enough, Joshua met half the swim team as he was going into the store.

"I'll be right out," he told them, and then emerged in only a few minutes.

"That didn't take long," one of his friends remarked.

"I just had to get a few things."

"Are you ready for the swim meet?" the captain of team asked.

"I think so, Charlie. I've been practicing every day. I hope we win."

"We should do well. We have a good team this year."

"I hate to leave you all, but I have to get right home. What I have is for supper and everything else is all ready. I'll see you tomorrow at the pool."

Supper was almost ready, except for the corn. The water was boiling. Joshua husked the corn and put it in the pot of boiling water. Noticing that his father was still resting under the cherry tree, he went out quietly and sat on a chair next to him, and waited till he opened his eyes.

"Abba, are you all right?"

"Why do you ask that, Son?"

"Because I rarely see you resting like this."

"Joshua, for a young boy, you sure do a lot of worrying. You have to learn to trust God."

"I do trust God, Abba, but I also care very much for those I love, and it's not easy to be detached from what happens to them. Sometimes you look so tired. What would Mother do without you? Life would not be the same. It would be so painful. My heart pains for people who lose loved ones, especially for children who lose parents."

"Don't worry about things like that. There is still much work to be done, and God won't take me home until my work is finished, and that won't be until you are old enough to take care of Mother. So, be at peace and enjoy being a child."

"Child, Abba? I'm almost eleven years old. And if God isn't going to take you home until your work is done, then don't work so fast."

Joseph laughed hard at his precocious child.

Then Joshua said, "Tomorrow we are having our swimming meet. Would you like to come? I'm going to be in it, but I don't think I'm a very good swimmer. I practice a lot, but I'm not much better than when I started."

"Joshua, your mother and I would love to watch you swim, even if you don't win."

"I don't know whether we'll win, but I think we have a good chance to win some of the events. Some of the other kids on the team are really good."

"Your mother and I will be there, Son."

That night all that Joshua could think of was the swim meet. He enjoyed life and put all he had into everything he did. His last thoughts that night were his prayers to his "Father in heaven." He really pestered his Father in heaven to help his teammates do well. He would like his team to win, but playing well was better. As God is very real to some children, he was very real to Joshua as well. Talking to him was a fun part of his life, but something too personal and too beautiful to share with anyone else.

The next day arrived. The swim meet started late. One of the boys lived quite a distance away and had a difficult time finding a ride to Shadybrook. The competition went on for a good three hours. Joshua's team did well. Even Joshua was not as bad as he thought he was. In fact, he was excellent in the relay, and in the distance swimming he came in first. Sheer determination rather than skill helped him in that.

In the five competitions, his team came in first place in one, second place in two, fourth place in one, and third place in another. It seems everybody won something, so they all left happy. Miss Cashin was happy she let Joshua be part of the swim team in exchange for helping her with tasks around the pool. She called him aside afterward and told him she was proud of all that he had accomplished in such a short time. Joshua beamed from ear to ear, especially since his mother and father were standing nearby and heard what she had said to him.

On his way home with his parents, Joshua told them about the lady letting him play on the team and use the pool if he would help her with work that had to be done.

"We became good friends," Joshua told them.

"Is there anyone who is not your friend, Joshua?" his father asked him jokingly.

"There are some I like more than others, and if someone doesn't like me, I try to be nice anyway. It's not always easy, but I try. Some kids don't have a happy life at home like we do. They're the ones who are sometimes difficult, but when I think of how they're hurting, I try to understand and be nice. But sometimes, when someone is really mean, I become very upset. It's hard for me to be nice to them, but I try."

"Joshua, do you realize that next week school starts and you will be going to class every day?" his mother said to him. "Do you have everything ready?"

"I think so. I do have to get some supplies. I'll make a list for when we go shopping. I don't need much."

"Are you looking forward to school?" Joseph asked him.

"Yes, Abba, it will be fun. I'll meet all new friends, and I have a lot of questions to ask the teachers."

"Like what, Son?"

"Like why there are so many poor people on earth when

my Father in heaven has given so much to rich people so they could share with others his generosity to them, and why are there wars, where God's children slaughter one another."

"You worry about things like that, too, my son?" his mother asked him.

"Yes, Mother, all the time. I feel other people's pain."

"I don't think your teachers are going to be able to answer questions like that."

"Well, I will ask the them anyway, because I think it's important for us to think about things like that."

His parents looked at each other and smiled.

7

J OSHUA FOUND HIMSELF IN THE FIFTH GRADE. THERE were almost thirty new potential friends, which was his first thought as he glanced around the room. Some of them he knew from the baseball and swim teams. Most were strangers. He looked around to see if his friend Marguerite was in the class. Then he remembered that she was younger, so she was probably in the third grade.

"Hi, Joshua," some of his friends called out to him when they noticed him. Joshua looked across the room and returned their greeting, then sat in one of the few remaining desks. He felt proud to be in the fifth grade. He was also proud of his new clothes, which his mother had made, but Joshua knew that his mother was an artist when it came to designing and fashioning clothes. He was not at all ashamed. He thought his pants and shirt were, as the kids would say, "cool" or "awesome." In fact, one girl remarked that they looked like a new designer style. His mother had even embroidered a little shepherd boy on the shirt pocket. The collar did not fold down. It was just a stiff band with an inch opening in the front. There were three buttons down the front. The bottom half of the shirt was one piece, so it had to be put on over the head. Joshua knew it was a well-designed piece of work. He was proud to say his mother had made it.

"Do you think she would design clothes for us if we asked her?" a girl asked Joshua.

"I think she might, but she's awfully busy most of the time. You'd have to ask her. I know she'd be very gracious."

The teacher called the class to order, and from the class register called out the names of the students: Ruth Abriel, Joan Allard, William Bannon, Helen Bartlett, Kathleen Begley, Allan Boudreau, Doris Calkins, Mary Clausey, Marie Crowley, Anna Harrington, Donald Lantz, Claire Lawlor, Emma Lee, Irene Morini, Lois Nevin, Winifred O'Rourke, Harriet Reuter, Irene Scarff, "and the new boy in our school, Joshua Ben-Yacob." Some of Joshua's more boisterous friends let out a typical "Yeh, yeh, Joshua!"—much to Joshua's embarrassment when he saw that the teacher was taken aback by the outburst.

"Joshua, you are the new boy in the class this year. I know most of the others, more by reputation than from being their teacher. I can tell you already fit in quite well with them all. They're good students, a little rambunctious at times, but good nonetheless. I know most of their parents. Welcome to our class, Joshua. Where did you live before you moved to Shadybrook?"

"We lived near Washington, ma'am," Joshua answered politely.

"The state?"

"No, the city."

"We all welcome you, Joshua. Hopefully, I'll get a

chance to meet your parents someday. They must be nice people to have raised such a well-mannered boy."

"Thank you, ma'am."

"Well, you are all welcome to my class. I'm sure you all know my name already. In case some of you forgot over the summer, my name is Miss Axeman. Your teachers have all told me that I'm lucky to have you as my students. I'm sure we are going to have an exceptional year with all of us working together. First order of business is the format of your homework papers. I know many of you students print. This year it's important that we all learn how to do cursive. So, all homework papers must be written in cursive. I know you've learned it in previous classes, so it's not new to you. But, it's important that you're able to write in cursive. It makes a much better impression on people who you'll have to do business with later on. So, for your own benefit, I am going to be very strict on that."

"Miss Axeman, what does cursive mean?"

The class did not know whether Joshua was serious or being a comedian, but there was dead silence. Even Miss Axeman was caught off-guard.

"Joshua, I assume you've never learned cursive. Words in books are printed. Cursive is the flowing style with each letter connected to each other, like this."

With that she wrote Joshua's name on the blackboard in cursive, then asked if he had learned to write like that.

"No, I never did, but I will learn how to by tomorrow if you show me."

The whole class laughed, much to Joshua's chagrin.

"I'll show you after class, Joshua," the teacher said, "then you can practice when you go home. That will be your homework for tonight."

The first day of school went by fast. The teacher took

Joshua aside at the end of the day and showed him how to write cursive. As soon as he got home he could not wait to practice his cursive. Over and over and over he wrote his name and the sentences the teacher had given him for practice.

"Joshua, did the teacher give you all that homework to do on your first day?" Miriam asked.

"Not really, Mother. I'm practicing my cursive. The other students know cursive. I never heard of it, so I have to learn it if I want to keep up with the class. I think I can do it, now that I've been practicing."

Joshua practiced until suppertime, then immediately after supper until bedtime. At bedtime, he asked his mother if his cursive looked neat. She looked at his paper and was surprised that he had been able to learn it so quickly.

"That is excellent, Son. I am sure the teacher will be happy with what you have accomplished in only one night."

Joshua felt proud of himself, even though the flow of his script was not even, nor the letters perfect. Practice would eventually take care of that. The sentences were, however, clear enough to read and understand. He went to bed with a good feeling that he had accomplished something that was not easy, but which he had been able to do, as he'd promised Miss Axeman.

The next day at school, Joshua could not wait for his teacher to ask to see his paper and what he had accomplished in his homework. He wanted to show it to her before she asked, but he thought it better if he was more modest about what he had accomplished. It wasn't until the end of the first period during a break that she asked Joshua to bring his homework up to her desk so she could look at it and see how well he had done.

Joshua was very excited. As soon as the break started,

Joshua brought up his paper. Miss Axeman looked at it and looked at Joshua. "Are you sure you haven't done cursive before?"

"Yes, Miss Axeman. I never did cursive before. I practiced ever since I went home yesterday."

"Well, it's not perfect, but I can tell that the person who did this is very familiar with cursive. Did your parents help you with this?"

Joshua was crushed, first of all that this teacher, whom he was beginning to like, questioned his honesty, but also because he had worked so hard hoping she would be pleased with what he had accomplished in so short a time.

"No, Miss Axeman. My parents don't know cursive. They only write Hebrew."

"Well, young man, I would be less than honest if I said I believed that you did this."

"And I, too, would be less than honest if I said I did not do it. I don't tell lies," Joshua said firmly, not used to people questioning his honesty.

The teacher dropped the matter, but she kept the paper and put it in her desk drawer. Joshua wondered what she intended to do with it. Crestfallen and hurt that the teacher thought he was being dishonest, he walked back to his desk and sat down while the others were still chatting. One of Marguerite's friends, Annie, came over to him and asked why he looked sad, and what had happened.

Joshua smiled and was reluctant to complain about the teacher not believing him. He merely said that the teacher was looking over his homework, and wanted to look at it some more. Joshua was not one to complain or look for sympathy. He did want to settle the issue, so he decided to write a note in cursive to the teacher. It read, "Dear Miss Axeman, You made me feel proud that you thought my cursive writing was very nice for a person who was not familiar with cursive. It was very difficult when I first started but it got easier as I continued practicing. Hopefully, I will improve as I practice more." It was signed, "Joshua Ben-Yousef, your student."

The note showed sensitivity for a young boy because Joshua knew the teacher would find out that he really did the writing, and this would save her the embarrassment of having to apologize for not believing him. It also made the teacher think that Joshua wasn't offended but felt proud that she thought his writing was so good for a first-time try at something so difficult. He put the note on the teacher's desk at the end of class, knowing that as soon as the class had filed out, she would go back and clear off her desk.

No sooner were they outside the classroom than his friends interrogated him as to what had happened when the teacher looked at his paper. All Joshua would say was that the teacher thought his writing was nicely done for a first try. They laughed as they concluded that Joshua's first attempt was not really that good and the teacher was being nice.

"Joshua, what are you doing this afternoon?" one of the boys asked.

"If my father needs me to help him, I'll work with him for a while. If he doesn't need me, I'll be free."

"Would you like to hike up the cliff and see the cave? It's awesome."

"Gee, that would be fun. Who's going?"

"About five of us: Mike, George, Jimmy, Charlie, and John MacIntosh. If you can come, we're going to meet at the pizza place in half an hour. If you're not there, we'll know you had to work. See you later."

Joshua's father was in the back of the yard, kneeling in the vegetable garden, pulling weeds.

"Need some help, Dad?" Joshua asked as he walked over to his father and put his hand affectionately on his shoulder.

"Oh, school's out already? How did your teacher like your homework?"

"She thought it was good for a first try. Need some help with the garden?"

"You might want to do the weeds in the flower garden in front of the house. They're getting pretty thick. It won't take too long, then you can be free."

"Good, my friends want me to go with them to the cave on the top of the cliff."

"They're all good boys, aren't they, Son?"

"Yes, Dad. You don't have to worry about that. I have to meet them in about half an hour."

"You should be finished weeding in plenty of time."

Joshua ran into the house, knowing that his mother would be in the kitchen either cooking or baking.

"Hi, Mother," he said as he gave her a big hug and kissed her on both cheeks. "I missed you, Mother."

"I missed you, too, Joshua. Did the teacher like your homework?"

"I think so. It was so good she thought maybe you helped me."

Miriam laughed. "Don't worry; she'll soon learn it was your work."

"I did tell her that you write in Hebrew. She thought it was good for my first try. I guess she wondered if I really did it. Later on I wrote her a note and left it on her desk, so now she knows for sure that I wrote it. I like Miss Axeman; she's a nice lady, and she's pretty. Mother, I have to rush to do the weeding out front; then, if it's okay, I'd like to go with my friends up to see the cave at the top of the cliff."

"Who's going?"

"Just the kids you know. They're all good kids, so don't worry."

"Have a good time, and be careful!"

The hike up the cliff was fun. Along the trail they unknowingly surprised a flock of turkeys, which took flight with such a loud noise, it frightened them. They had never seen a turkey fly, and so many of them taking off all at once made a terrible racket. When they finally reached the top, they looked around at the breathtaking view. The whole valley opened up, and they could see almost seventy miles to the north and east. They all stood there in wonder and felt like they were on the top of the world, which they really were in that spot.

"Let's look for the cave," Mike said. "I have never seen it. Where is it?"

George pointed in the direction of the cave, telling the others it was only about four or five hundred feet away. He had been there before with other friends. After looking through brush and small trees and thornbushes, they finally found the entrance.

"Gee, it's dark in there," Mike said.

"I have a flashlight," Charlie said. "I hope the batteries are good."

George was the first to enter, with the others following.

"Mike, bring the flashlight up here," George called back to him.

The cave was not very wide, perhaps, ten to twelve feet, but seemed to go quite far into the mountain. At one point a huge number of bats shocked them as they suddenly flew past and out the mouth of the cave. The floor of the cave was flat and smooth and easy to walk on, though it was slippery because of the moisture. Soon they came to a divide and wondered if they should go farther. They decided that if they stayed together, it would be safe. They continued straight ahead, since it seemed to be the main section of the cave, but it soon took a left turn and, not far ahead, it split again. At that point they all started to get frightened, but George reassured them that he knew the way. Taking the opening going to the right, they walked nearly a hundred feet and heard water flowing. Shining the flashlight ahead, they realized they had come to a ledge with a sharp drop-off. The sound of water was coming from a waterfall on the far side of a big hole. As exciting as it was, the boys were really scared now, and everyone decided they better turn back.

It did not take long before they reached the point where the cave split into two tunnels. "Which one shall we take," Charlie asked, "the one on the right?"

"No," Joshua said, "we came in from the one on the left."

No one could agree, and at that point one of the boys started to cry. "We're lost and we'll never get out of here. We'll be buried in here."

"Stop crying," George ordered. "We're not lost. We just have to keep a cool head and figure out what to do."

Joshua made a suggestion. "I know we came from the left passageway. I am sure of that. Remember, when we came down and we could turn either left or right, and we decided to turn right. Well, that's where we are, except now we're going in the opposite direction, so we have to go left."

Not everyone agreed.

"Well, I'll tell you what we can do. I will stay right here and will not move. If you all go down the left section and keep going, you should see the light at the entrance. Count to one hundred and fifty slowly. By that time you should be able to see light. Then come back and get me. I'll be right here."

They agreed that would be the best and the safest way to go, so they started on their way back.

"Don't forget to come back and get me," Joshua called out to them after they had walked some distance away.

"We won't, Joshua. Hope you're not afraid of the dark," one of them yelled back.

As soon at the others were out of earshot, Joshua noticed how dark it was. He could see nothing, and started to become frightened.

"Father in heaven, I'm scared. I can't see anything in here. Now that there's no light, I can't even tell where the two sections of the cave begin. If I stand just the way I am, I think the right section is just to my right, and the passageway the boys took is just to my left, I think. Father, I'm really scared. Please help me not to get lost in here. I don't know how I'll ever get out."

It seemed like hours were passing even though it had been only about ten minutes. There was still no sound from the boys. Actually, they had reached the entrance to the cave, but when they got there, Mike told the others that the flashlight had gone out. The batteries were dead.

"I'm not going back in there without a light," Charlie said. Then they all said the same thing.

"What are we going to do about Joshua? We can't just leave him in there," George said.

At that point they panicked and could not come to any kind of a decision. It took at least fifteen minutes before John MacIntosh made a suggestion. "There are five of us. I will go into the cave first, and Mike will hold my hand but stay behind me. That will get us about five feet in, and then Charlie will hold Mike's hand and that will give us another few feet. Then, Jimmy will hold Charlie's hand and that will give us another couple of feet. Then George can hold Jimmy's hand, which will give us a total of about twenty feet. Then we can walk farther into the cave in a straight line, knowing that the entrance is right behind us. If we keep holding each other's hand, we can't lose each other, and we know that all we have to do is turn around and, while holding hands, we can find our way out again." They all agreed to the plan and started walking back into the dark hole.

In the meantime, Joshua realized something must have gone wrong, so he knew he had better try to feel his way along the wall of the cave. From where he was standing, he could feel where the cave split. He knew he had to go left, so he started on his way. He fell a couple of times and slipped on a puddle of water, but continued moving ahead. It was slow because he could see nothing. He called to the others but there was no response. He became even more frightened.

"Father in heaven, please help me find my way. I know I should trust you, but I can't help being scared. It's so dark and I can't see a thing."

Finally, he thought he heard the sound of voices.

"Hello! Hello!" he called out. "Are you all there?"

For a moment there was no answer, then he heard his name. "Joshua, can you hear us? We're coming back in but we have no flashlight, but you were right. It is just a straight line out of here. Just keep coming. We'll keep talking so you can tell you are coming toward us."

Joshua felt relief. He kept feeling his way along the wall as he could hear the voices becoming louder and clearer.

"Thank you, Abba, thank you for watching over us, and for helping me get out of here."

Suddenly John MacIntosh let out a bloodcurdling scream,

not realizing that Joshua had reached the group in the dark and reached out and happened to grab MacIntosh's shoulder.

"It's only me!" Joshua called out.

"Don't ever do anything like that again. I thought someone else was in here, and he was going to drag me into the black cave."

"Now, how do we get out of here?" Charlie asked.

"If we keep holding each other's hands, we can backtrack, and get back to the entrance," John MacIntosh assured them. "Joshua, you hold on to my hand!"

As Joshua grabbed John's hand, the group started on its way out, not totally convinced they were really going to find their way out. But in no time at all they reached the entrance and heaved a huge sigh of relief.

After relaxing for a minute and cracking jokes to break the tension, they started on their way home.

"Were you scared in that dark cave all alone, Joshua?" Charlie asked.

"Was I scared? I tried not to be, but it was so dark, I was afraid of everything. I knew if I stood still, all I had to do is go straight ahead into the left tunnel. So I was afraid to move for fear of losing which way I would be heading. I really prayed hard. I know God watches over us, but I was still scared."

Darkness was beginning to settle over the woods and the path became difficult to see, but they were not far from open space, so they just kept moving straight ahead until they reached the clearing.

"That's the last time I'm going in that cave. That was really scary," George said.

"That's my last time. I know that for sure," Jimmy added. "I was never so scared in all my life."

Reaching the center of the village, Joshua asked if they

would like to come to his house for something to eat before they went home. "My mother makes good cookies, and homemade soda, which is delicious."

"Okay, that would be fun. Your mother is a real nice lady. She's pretty, too," John said.

When Joshua reached home with his crew of friends and went inside, his mother took one look at him and, in shock, asked him what had happened.

"Why, Mother?"

"You are all dirty. Did you fall? Did you get hurt?"

"Mother, I'm okay. Nothing happened. We just got lost in the cave."

"You mean a real cave, a big one?"

"Yes, really big, and the flashlight went out. The battery went dead. But, Mother, I know I should have asked you first, but I brought all my friends home with me to have some soda. I hope you don't mind."

"No, Son, have them come in. Don't leave them standing outside. They are always welcome."

"Do you have any of that homemade soda?" Joshua asked as he went to call his friends into the kitchen.

"There's plenty in the refrigerator."

"Gee, this is a nice kitchen," Mike said as they plowed through the doorway. "You should have seen it before, when we used to sneak in here, because everybody said it was a haunted house."

Joseph came into the kitchen, rubbing his eyes. He had apparently been snoozing in the living room until the talking woke him up.

"Welcome, boys!"

"Hello, Mr. Ben-Yousef," George said, thinking that must be his name since it was Joshua's last name, and not knowing that the last name changes from father to son. Joshua's last name was Ben-Yousef, which means "son of Joseph." "You really did a beautiful job rebuilding this house. You're a genius. This place used to be a haunted house, and everybody was afraid to come near it. Now it is beautiful."

Joseph helped his wife move the table away from the wall so everyone could sit around and relax. As Joshua poured the soda into glasses and brought the tray over to the table, Miriam put out the platter of cookies she had baked just a short time before, intending them to be a surprise for supper.

Though it was not very thoughtful of Joshua to bring his friends in at suppertime, his mother was gracious and said nothing, though she was thinking what the other mothers must be wondering when their sons did not come home.

One of the boys, however, remembered that it was time for dinner and commented that he would have to be leaving, as his mother would be waiting for him.

"We can finish our cookies first," Charlie said. "These cookies are good, Mrs. Ben-Yacob," he said. "I wish my mother would make cookies like these. The soda's good, too, even better than Pepsi and Coke. You could make a lot of money if you sold it."

"Thank you. I am glad you like it."

George started to get up and the others followed. "I have to get home. I forgot it was suppertime, and my mother will be upset, wondering what happened to me. Thank you so much for the snack. It was delicious."

They all agreed and started filing out of the house.

"See you tomorrow, Joshua. Thanks for the treat, and for remembering the way out of the cave," John said.

"And for staying in there by yourself so we could find our way out," Mike added.

After the boys left, Miriam asked Joshua if he would put

the glasses in the sink and set the table while she took out the food being kept warm in the oven.

"Oh, I'm sorry, Mother. I forgot what time it was. I shouldn't have brought everybody here at suppertime."

"Joshua, I am glad you enjoy your friends, but next time, think beforehand. Your friends had to be home for supper as well."

Joseph said nothing, but Joshua realized he must be hungry after working hard all day. He apologized.

"Forget it, Son. I got a good nap while I was waiting. Now, after that rest I'm so hungry I could eat a camel."

"I'm hungry, too. That was some hike," Joshua exclaimed.

Miriam said nothing, but Joshua could tell she was brooding over something.

When all the food was on the table, they all sat down and said their little prayer. Miriam asked Joshua if he would pour the water. Joseph watched him carefully this time. Joshua knew he was watching.

Miriam passed the food to her husband, and when he finished, passed it to Joshua, who always insisted that his mother take hers first. He was already stuffing his mouth with the homemade bread, which he loved.

As they started eating, Miriam asked Joshua what the boys meant when they were leaving.

Joshua knew that was what was bothering her. As soon as the boys said it, he knew his mother would remember it. And she did.

"Mother, it is nothing to worry about. The cave was a wonderful experience. We went in a long way and came to a beautiful waterfall. We were lucky one of the boys brought a flashlight, so we could see where we were going. But when we were leaving we got confused and could not tell which was the right way out.

"There was a fork in the cave. I knew which was the right way, but the others were not sure, so they could not agree which way to go. I told them I was sure which was the right way, and said I would stay at the fork while they took the road I suggested. If they found it was the right one, then they could come back and get me. If it was not the right one, they could come back and we would then take the other tunnel.

"But what happened was their flashlight went out, so they were afraid to come back in the dark to get me. I knew something must have happened, so I started walking out myself, and met them almost halfway. Then we all got out. There was no need to be worried, Mother."

"I didn't realize it was a big cave like that or I would not have let you go. You all could have gotten lost in there. Weren't you scared?"

Joshua did not want to admit he was scared, but finally confessed, "Yes, Mother, I was scared stiff. I knew I shouldn't have been. I wanted to trust my Father in heaven, but I still couldn't stop being scared. I prayed hard. But here I am, Mother, and see, there was no reason to worry."

While the two were talking, Joseph was trying to figure out what had happened to his glass of water again. He knew Joshua had poured water this time. He watched him. And it was water when it went into his glass. But when he took the first sip, he knew something had happened to it. It was wine again, and good wine. He looked at Joshua and caught him watching him, and immediately knew something was up, but for the life of him he could not figure out what had happened.

"I have to admit, this is good wine, Miriam."

"What on earth are you talking about, dear?" she said with shocked surprise.

"Maybe you don't know, but something funny has happened to my water again, and I am not imagining things. This was water when the kid poured it. But here, you taste it."

Miriam tasted it and immediately looked at Joshua, who was totally absorbed in eating his supper. He did not even lift his head. She said nothing, but was wondering many things as she gave the glass back to Joseph.

"It *is* good wine, much better than what I get at the store."

"This lamb is so-o good, Mother. I love it," Joshua finally commented, hoping it would change the subject.

"Thank you, Joshua. I know you both like lamb. By the way, Son, don't you have homework tonight?"

"No. Last night was special. Only I had homework so I could practice my cursive. I don't think we will have our next homework until tomorrow night."

"Do you like school, Joshua?" Joseph asked him.

"Yes, very much. I like my friends, and I like to learn new things. I also like my teacher. She's nice. She's pretty, too."

"I don't think it would be a good idea for you to go up to that cave again, Joshua. It sounds too dangerous. Even if you are careful, some of the others may not be, and something tragic could happen." This was Joseph's firm way of speaking, with the tone of voice that Joshua knew would not tolerate discussion. So he wisely said nothing, other than, "Yes, Dad."

CHAPTER

8

THE NEXT MORNING THREE OF JOSHUA'S FRIENDS did not show up for school. As the students were gathering outside waiting to go inside, Joshua saw Jimmy and asked where the others were.

"They were too tired to get up today," he told him. "My mother was talking to George's mother, who said that her son was exhausted, and you know the way mothers talk, they found out that the others were too tired to get out of bed. Now we'll all be interrogated about what we did that made everybody too tired to go to school."

"I already told my parents what we did, and I told them everything, so I don't have to worry about them questioning me," Joshua said.

"I told my parents we walked up the cliff and it was a big hike, so they already know," Jimmy confided. "But I didn't tell them about the cave, so when they find out from the others, I'm sure they'll get all worried and forbid us to go up there ever again."

"It probably wasn't very wise of us to go into that cave. That could have been dangerous. It sure was scary. I wouldn't ever want to go in there again," Joshua added.

"Me neither."

When Miss Axeman took the roll call and commented that three of the boys were absent, she casually mentioned that the boys' mothers had called to say they were "sick." Joshua and Jimmy looked across the aisle at each other and grinned, knowing that their friends were really too tired to get out of bed.

Later that day, Joshua ran into the others and casually expressed his sadness over their being sick, and hoped that they were feeling better. They all just laughed at Joshua's humor.

"I guess we won't be going to the cave anymore," George said. "Our mothers found out where we were, and that we almost got lost in the cave. They panicked and forbade us ever to go near the place again."

"What are we going to do for fun now?"

"I have an idea," Joshua said. "The pond down on the back road is really big. I found out that there is also a stream that runs off it. It's almost like a little river and runs down into another lake which is a lot bigger than the pond. Why don't we make a raft and float from the pond down the stream to the lake? That could be fun."

"Where are we going to get a raft?" Mike asked.

"We can make one out of tree trunks," Joshua replied.

"I've got a better idea. We have a big, heavy plastic raft in our garage," Jimmy added. "We can take that, and there's plenty of room for us all."

"That's great," George added, excited as he imagined another adventure in the offing.

"When are we going to do this?" Charlie asked.

"How about tomorrow?" Joshua suggested.

"That would be great. It will give me time to make sure the raft has no holes in it. And then we'll have to get it inflated."

"So, it looks like tomorrow it is," Jimmy said, and they all agreed.

They all went to sleep that night dreaming about the great adventure they were going to have traveling across the pond and downstream into the big lake. What an adventure that was going to be! They couldn't wait until the next day arrived and when school would be out.

Next morning at school, Miss Axeman intercepted Joshua as he was walking down the corridor. With a rather shy smile, she greeted him and in an apologetic tone said, "Joshua, thank you for the little note. It was very well written. You must be a very exceptional young man to have mastered cursive writing in such a short time."

"Thank you, Miss Axeman. I knew I had to catch up with the other students who had already learned it, so I worked hard at it. I am glad you liked it."

It still bothered her that she had insinuated that he had not done the work, and knew it must have offended him, so thinking she could make it up to him, she asked him to write a number of questions on the blackboard, which she directed the class to copy down and answer as part of their homework for that night. Though he wrote slowly and deliberately, it was carefully done and very readable. When he finished and went back down to his desk, he looked up at the board to view what he had written. He was proud of what he had done, though he could see it was still not perfect and needed improvement.

In history class, the teacher talked about the first colonists in Virginia and Massachusetts, and how they came to this country for religious freedom, because they were separatists.

"Miss Axeman, what does 'separatist' mean?" Joshua asked with a confused look.

The teacher was clearly caught up short and had to think of a way of explaining to a young boy what the Pilgrims and Puritans were all about. She finally came up with a short but precise answer. The separatists were Christians who had started their own version of religion.

Joshua still looked confused. "My parents told me that only God can start a religion. It is God's way of telling us how he wants us to worship him. Do separatists tell God how they are going to worship him?"

"Your parents sound like very intelligent people, Joshua, but this is a matter we cannot discuss in class. It is important that you believe what your parents teach you, Joshua."

History class was fascinating to Joshua because it was always about people and events in people's lives. It was very much like the stories his family always read in the scriptures, which Joshua always liked to hear when he was small and to read after he had learned to read.

Though most of the class never asked questions, Joshua's active mind always had questions he needed answered, and as soon as a question arose, up shot his hand.

When Miss Axeman told about the Indians and their relationship with the Pilgrims, and how the Pilgrims tried to convert the Indians to Christianity, Joshua wondered why they wanted to do that.

"Because they wanted the Indians to follow God's laws, and change them from their old pagan ways."

"But the Indians seem to have had a better understanding of God and his creation than the Pilgrims did. The Pilgrims seem like unhappy people."

"Joshua, I love the way your mind works and the questions you have, but I would never be able to answer them all. I will tell you what I will do. I will give you a list of books you can read, and if those books do not have answers to the questions you have, then you can ask me. Is that all right?"

"Yes, I think that will be a help, because I become restless if I have a question that has no answer."

By the look on the teacher's face, it was easy to see what she was thinking: "Thank God, I don't have too many inquisitive kids like that in my class," although one could see that she liked Joshua and it was a joy to have a student like him who was so eager to learn.

As each school day passed, Joshua's thirst to learn grew deeper, and when he was home he devoured the books the teacher had given him to read, though she had not realized that by giving him all that extra reading, she was not putting off his questions in class but giving him food for more questions. One example was why the colonists could not live in peace with the Indians, when the Indians were so willing to give so much of their land as a show of goodwill to the colonists. To Joshua's thinking, the Indians were more religious than the colonists because they were so close to nature, and their prayers seemed real, like they came from their hearts. The colonists' religion seemed make-believe, and made them act holy because they had to be holy.

ATER SCHOOL THE NEXT AFTERNOON, THEY ALL went to Jimmy's garage, got the raft, carried it to the gas station, filled it up, and trotted down to the pond, all ready for their trip down the "river."

The stream flowing from the pond was wider and deeper than they had thought, and much longer as well. It took them almost fifteen minutes to reach the end of the stream, and they were amazed to see the vast lake spread out before them. They had lived there all their lives and never gone that far. In fact, all they knew was that there was a stream that they thought was nothing more than the overflow from the pond. They never imagined it would lead to this lake, so well hidden in the woods, and alive with fish, good-sized ones judging by those that were darting almost a foot into the air.

"What a great place to fish!" Jimmy exclaimed excitedly.

"Yeah, look at the size of that one!" George shouted.

That one was over fifteen inches long. They all decided they would come down again and go fishing.

"But let's keep it a secret, otherwise everybody will be coming down here and it will be no fun," Mike said, to which everyone agreed.

The lake was at least ten acres in size, and the boys had one of the best times in their life just discovering it.

"Joshua, how did you ever find this place?" Charlie asked.

"I come down here to swim, and one day I decided to explore, so I walked around the edge of the pond and through the woods along the stream to see where it led. I noticed the stream kept getting wider and deeper, and then all of a sudden I saw this huge lake. I felt like a real explorer. I was so thrilled."

"Gee, thanks for telling us about it. You could have kept it a secret just for yourself," George said.

"That's no fun," Joshua said. "It's more fun when you can share with someone, especially your best friends."

"If we come fishing, though, we're going to have to get something else than this raft. We can't all fish from this raft," Mike commented.

"We'll think of something," Joshua said. "Maybe if you're all willing to help, my father might make a few small boats for us, something we can carry down with us, or maybe even hide in the woods."

"That would be great," George said excitedly. "When can we start?"

"I'll have to ask my father first. I know he's always very busy, but my father is my best friend, and I know he will help us."

"Oh!" Joshua said in sudden shock. "We haven't gone home from school yet. My parents will be all upset wondering what happened. We'd better get back."

"And my mother told me to come right home, too. She had to take me to the doctor this afternoon," Jimmy said with panic in his voice.

Knowing they were all in trouble, they didn't even wait to deflate the raft. They just carried it down the road and plopped it in Joshua's back yard to save time, and then went directly home.

"Where have you been, Joshua? We have been waiting for you since school ended." His mother was very upset, as Joshua could tell. So was his father, who did not have to say a word. At times like this Joshua wished his father would say something so he wouldn't have to worry about what was going on in his mind. He knew he was going to have to be punished for being inconsiderate.

All he could say was, "I'm really sorry. Some of my friends wanted to go down to the pond. We forgot all about coming home after school. We got all excited about exploring the pond and the big stream that goes into the huge lake." Then he realized it was the wrong time to tell them what a good time he was having with his friends.

He could tell his mother was upset not only because he did not come right home after school, but also because the supper she had all ready was now overcooked. He knew she liked to have everything perfect for supper as the evening meal was the important meal each day, the one everyone waited for all day long.

He also knew this was certainly not the time to ask his father if he could make the boats he had promised his friends. Not knowing what to say next, he thought it best to just stop talking, wash up without being told, and get ready for supper.

When Joshua left the kitchen, Joseph, realizing Miriam was disappointed about the supper's not being perfect, tried to calm her. "Miriam, I am sure the dinner will be perfect. Don't let it upset you. So what if it is not as perfect as you might like. I'm not a food expert. I love whatever you cook. If it's different from the way you cooked it another time, I just think you used a different recipe. I am upset with Joshua for not coming home after school. I am going to have to punish him for being thoughtless. I can't let him think he can be on his own and not be responsible. I could have used him this afternoon when I was working upstairs."

"I know, Joseph. He has always been so thoughtful, but these new friends of his are so close they can't wait until school is out, and they forget everything else. I know they are all good boys, but you're right; he has to learn to be responsible."

"All right, Son," Joseph said as Joshua entered the kitchen. "Let's all sit down and enjoy our supper. I know you're sorry, so I don't want to hear you say it again. Let's just enjoy supper, and you can tell your mother and me what you did all afternoon."

After the blessing, Joshua passed the food to his father, who took the platter without saying any more than a grumble, rather than the usual "Thank you, Son."

When Joshua took his first bite of food, he said, "Mother, this is delicious. I thought it would be ruined after my being late. But it's perfect."

"The boy's right, dear. It is delicious. It isn't overcooked or even dry. It *is* perfect."

"Now, Joshua, what did you do all afternoon?" Joseph asked.

"When we came out of school, I met my friends outside and one of them asked what we could do for fun. I said, 'Let's go down to the pond off the back road.' I told them about the stream that flows from it, and that we could explore it and see where it leads. Everybody got all excited about it, so we took off and went down exploring. And, Abba, you know what? There are some really big fish in the lake way down at the end of the stream. Maybe you and I can go fishing someday soon. I know it would be fun. Maybe even mother can come with us."

As Joseph did not seem very enthusiastic, Miriam broke the silence. "How big were the fish, Joshua?"

"At least this big, Mother," the boy said as he held his hands up and spread them almost two feet apart.

"That big, Son?" his father said with an unbelieving smile.

Joshua was happy to see his father smiling. He knew he wasn't too upset.

"Yes, Abba," he said as his hands came a little closer together, but not much. "I'm really not exaggerating. They are really this big. I could tell easily when they jumped out of the water. Even my friends were surprised at how big they were."

"Do you have homework tonight, Son?" Joseph asked him.

"No, Abba. The teacher did not give us any tonight."

"I would like you to study just the same. What is important about school is developing the habit of learning, and to become a habit it is necessary to learn not just for school, but to learn just for the sake of learning. So after you finish washing the dishes, you go to your room and study or read."

"Yes, Abba," Joshua said meekly, just happy to be getting off so easy for not coming home right after school.

At night before bed, Miriam always came up to Joshua's room to kiss him good night and talk with him for a few minutes. Those few minutes were special times for the boy, a time when he could share a secret, or, like on this occasion, apologize for coming home late. It was always easier to tell his mother he was sorry. His father was always serious, and Joshua got nervous when he had to face his father after doing something wrong.

"Joshua, your father was very worried when you did not come home this afternoon. He knows you are usually considerate, and when you did not come home, he was worried that something might have happened to you. I know he worries too much, but he knows how special you are and he feels so responsible for you. Now, first thing tomorrow morning, tell your father that you will be right home after school, so you can help him with his work. You offer to do that before he has to tell you."

"Yes, Mother," Joshua said as he hugged and kissed her good night.

"Good night, Son, and don't forget to talk to your Father in heaven."

"I never forget, Mother. I share everything with him, even when I do things I shouldn't."

"May the angels watch over you."

"And may they protect you and father."

Joshua did not like going to sleep troubled. And he was still concerned about causing his parents worry. He knew his Father in heaven was not happy with it, either, so he needed to talk to him.

When he prayed, he usually knelt at his bedside, but this time he was really tired, so as soon as his mother turned off the light as she left the room, he poured his heart out. "Father in heaven, I know you are not happy with the way things went today. I was not very considerate, and even though I know you understand, I am sorry for the worry I caused my mother and father. Bless them, Father, and take away the pain I caused them. I don't want them to worry.

"I think my father may not be well, and even though he

doesn't say anything or complain, I notice he has to rest a lot, and today I should have come home right away from school so I could help him. Rushing out of school and seeing my friends distracted me, and going out to explore was so much fun.

"Father, I love you. I think of you all the time. I am learning things about myself that sometimes frighten me, like at the dinner table, and I know a glass of wine would help my father more than a glass of water, and then it happens. And, when I went swimming that time and I started walking on top of the water. Even though these things are fun, they make me nervous, Father. And when I can tell beforehand when something is going to happen to someone, and then it happens, it makes me feel funny.

"My mother told me you gave me these gifts and that I should appreciate them and not be afraid of them, but I still feel uncomfortable. Please, Father, help me to understand. Good night, Father, and thank you for your love, and for all you have done for me. And please bless my parents, and all my friends, and . . . even those who are not my friends."

In no time he was sound asleep.

NEXT MORNING A BEAUTIFUL SPRAY OF FLOWERS was set on the kitchen table. Joshua said nothing, but his mother made a big fuss over the thoughtfulness of whoever put them there. Joseph looked at Joshua and when their eyes met, Joshua blurted out, "Father, I'll be right home this afternoon so I can help you with your work."

"That would be nice, Son. I was just going to mention that, but I guess your mother already did."

Miriam blushed immediately, as she realized that her husband knew she had said something to Joshua about what he had discussed with her the night before. She quickly turned the subject back to the flowers. "Those flowers are so beautiful. How thoughtful! Pretty flowers always brighten up our spirits. Now if you both sit down, I will serve breakfast to the two favorite men in my life. Joshua, before you sit down, will you pour the orange juice?"

"Flowers may brighten up some people's spirits, but the

smell of breakfast is what picks up my spirits," Joseph commented. "And smelling the breakfast all the way upstairs was all I needed to start the day off right. Miriam, I have to admit, you sure do know the way to a man's heart."

"Yes, dear, right through his stomach," she quipped. "And I guess you know it's the sausage you made the other day that you smelled cooking. I couldn't resist tasting one before. These are the best."

As Joshua filled the glasses, his mother served the sausages and fried potatoes and omelets, and then put the pot of coffee on the table and sat down as they all thanked God for each other and for all the good things in their lives.

Joshua offered the platter to his mother, who gestured toward his father.

"Here, Abba, I will hold it for you."

"Thank you, Son."

Then he offered it to his mother.

"Take yours, Joshua."

As Joshua took a bite of the sausage, he looked at his father and excitedly burst out, "This sausage is delicious, Abba. Will you teach me how to do it, so I can make them when I get older? This is better than the kind you buy in the store."

"Thank you, Son. The next time I make some, I will show you how to do it. I make them so they are healthful and taste good as well. One of the reasons why they are so tasty is the way your mother cooks them. It makes a big difference how you cook them. I tried to cook them once and they didn't taste the same."

Joshua gobbled down his breakfast and, after kissing his parents, rushed out to school so he could see his friends before classes started.

"Joshua!" a girl's voice called out.

Turning around, he was surprised to see Marguerite, whom he hadn't seen since the beginning of school.

"Marguerite, I haven't seen you in weeks. What class are you in?"

"I'm in Mrs. Kane's class." She didn't want to say the third grade. It might sound like she was just a child and too young for Joshua to be her friend.

"I hope you're still my friend, even though we don't see each other that often since school started," Joshua said.

"I will always be your friend. I hope I see you again."

"You will. Do you like school?"

"I like some of the classes. I like writing and history. It's interesting, but I have trouble with numbers. I like to draw, so art class is fun. I'll draw you a picture someday."

"Great."

As Joshua's buddies approached, Marguerite walked away to meet her friends, who were walking up the street.

Talking about different subjects made Joshua think about his own interests and the things he was good at. He liked math. It was precise. It was accurate. It made sense. Math applied to everything. He was good at math even though it was still simple fifth grade math. He looked at some of his friends' seventh grade math and he could understand that, too. It looked so easy.

Out of curiosity, he had gone into the library one day to look at other math books. They had all seemed so easy to understand. Then he began to get frightened again. He had wanted so much to be like the others, and now he was becoming even more aware that he *was* different.

"Father in heaven, I don't want to be different. Why can't I just be like the others?"

He thought he heard a faint voice telling him, "Son, you

are different. You are special to me, and you must be prepared. Do not fear. One day you will understand."

Joshua could not tell whether he had really heard a voice or whether it was just his imagination. All through school that day he was preoccupied with what he was learning about himself. He was also beginning to notice that his Father in heaven was becoming more real to him. It was comforting, but also frightening because it was so new and made him feel even more different. He thought of asking some of his friends he felt closest to if they felt close to their Father in heaven. If they felt the same way, that would make him feel as if he were not too different after all. He could not wait until classes ended so he could ask his friend Jimmy if he talked to his Father in heaven. He would be the easiest to talk to about it.

So as soon as he left school that afternoon, he looked for Jimmy and, after finding him, the two walked down the street together.

"Joshua, did you ask your father if he would make the boats for us?"

"No, I did not think it was the right time to bring up the subject. I was so late for supper I didn't even want to mention the subject. Maybe I'll get a chance to ask him today. I'm going to be helping him with his work. I think he will say yes. Jimmy, speaking of fathers, do you talk to your Father in heaven?"

"Father in heaven?" Jimmy said in shock. "Who's that? I don't have a Father in heaven. My father is at work. He lives in the house with us. Why are you asking such a question? Did you think my father was dead?"

"No, no, Jimmy. I was just thinking about praying, I guess."

"Oh, that's different. I guess I pray sometimes. My family's not very religious. But when I have a test or when I have to go to the doctor, I might pray. But that's about it. Why, do you pray?"

"Yeah, I always had a feeling that God is always close by, so I talk to him."

"That's different. I never heard of that before," Jimmy said.

When Jimmy said "different," it was like an electric shock. He could not help concluding, "So there it is again. I *am* different."

Joshua became silent, and Jimmy asked him if he was okay.

"I'm okay, Jimmy. I just have to figure some things out. I'm learning a lot of new things since I came to Shadybrook and since school started, and I have to understand what it all means. I think why I like you, Jimmy, is because you are uncomplicated and have the goodness and innocence of a child."

"Joshua, I'm not a child," Jimmy said in a mildly protesting voice.

"Jimmy, I know you are not a child. I did not mean it that way, but you still have the innocence and wonder that children have. That is what makes you so open and honest, and I am happy that you are my friend. I can trust you."

"Joshua, you can always trust me. I am glad you are my friend, too. You are my best friend."

"Thank you, Jimmy."

By that time they had reached Mud Puddle Road, and they parted.

Joseph was sitting on the front porch when Joshua came jauntily down the street, singing a simple tune.

"You seem happy today, Son," Joseph said as he greeted him.

"I am happy, Father. I came right home so I can help you."

"Today is too nice a day to work, Joshua. Besides, I'd really like to catch one of those big fish you told me about. Would you like to go fishing?"

"I'd love to, Father. I'll run in and put on my old clothes, and be right out."

Joseph finished putting together the fishing pole he had made for his son. Whatever kind of wood he used was strong but flexible and had a good snap to it. It was perfect for a fishing pole. The line must have been real fishing line he had once bought from a hardware store. The reel was handmade, put together from parts he had in his workshop. It was clever. The pole he made for himself was like Joshua's, except Joshua's was smaller, and easier for him to handle.

Miriam walked out the door after Joshua came running out, smiling at the two of them. She was glad they could have fun together. But she worried about her husband's working so hard and not taking time to rest.

"You two be careful. I hope you have luck. If you do, we can have fish for supper."

Joseph was surprised to see how big the pond was.

"But, Father, that is not where we want to fish. It is the big lake. We have to walk through the woods to get there."

"Why can't we fish in the pond?"

"I never saw any fish here. But I know there are fish in the big lake, and we're sure to catch some. If we walk along the edge of the stream over there, we can walk down to the lake."

Joseph did not realize how far they would have to walk.

"How did you boys find the lake?"

"We used a raft that my friend Jimmy had in his garage, and we paddled all the way down the stream to the lake."

Walking that far along the shore of the stream was taxing the father, especially as Joshua was in a hurry to reach the lake.

"Joshua, I think we have to rest a while. I didn't realize it was such a long hike," Joseph said as he wiped his face, dripping with sweat, and sat down on a large fallen tree trunk.

Joshua walked a few yards away to a three-foot-high rocky bank. A steady stream of water flowed from between the stones. Joshua cupped his hands to hold the water, which he carefully brought to his father to drink.

"Joshua, you are so thoughtful. Thank you, Son. How do you know it is good water?"

"Because it is always cold and always running. I always drink it, so I know it's good."

"That seems to make sense. It tastes good, too."

Joshua brought some more for his father and then took some himself.

"Joshua, if we're going to fish down here, I think it would be easier if we made a little boat, maybe a sailboat, big enough so your mother could come along with us, and we could even have a little picnic after we fish."

At the mention of the boat, Joshua's eyes widened.

"Father, that would be great, but how would we get it down here?"

"I would have to make a set of wheels so we could pull it down the street to the pond and then just lift it off at the shore. That would be easy."

"And I could help you, too, and learn how to make a boat. Then I could make one for my friends for when we all go down to the lake together."

Joseph just listened, but was wondering about all of Joshua's friends. He knew a few of them, but some new ones he did not know at all, and he was concerned about what kind of boys they were.

"Well, let's get started, Son, or we'll never get back in time for supper," Joseph said as he got up from the log and picked up his fishing pole.

When they reached the lake, Joseph was shocked to see such a large body of water so close by. Seeing his father's surprise, Joshua could not contain his own enthusiasm.

"See, Father, I told you it was a big lake, and even we were surprised when we found it. It is a perfect place to fish. Wait till you see."

A short way along, there was a small beach formed by the deer and other animals coming daily to drink and walk in the cool water.

"Joshua, this is quite a lake. We are going to have fun," Joseph said as he took off his shoes and socks and rolled up his pant cuffs.

Joshua did the same, and after putting bait on their hooks, they both walked into the water.

"You walk down a ways, Son, so we don't catch one another rather than the fish. I'll stay here."

Walking out into the cool water was very refreshing for the tired, weary carpenter. He could have used this as a place to rest after working so hard on the house the past few months in the dangerously hot weather.

After almost twenty minutes, Joshua felt disappointed that neither of them had caught anything. He was hoping that his father would have at least caught something. After a few minutes more, and looking at the water near where his father was standing, Joshua called out to him.

"Abba, if you throw your line over to the left, I think there is a real big fish there."

"Son, there is nothing over there. I was just casting there and I didn't even get a bite."

"Abba, please try again. I know there's a big fish there."

Joseph cast his line over to his left and sure enough, hardly had it hit the water than the pole bent violently and almost pulled Joseph off balance. He went down on one knee and went down even more deeply into the cold water before he caught himself and was able to brace himself so he could start winding in the line.

The tug on the line was exciting. Joshua watched and got all excited as he saw the fun his father was having. This man, always so serious and thoughtful, had all of a sudden become a little kid again. Joshua laughed out loud.

"Father, you're funny. You're really having a lot of fun, aren't you?"

"I am, Son. I haven't had fun like this in such a long time. We have to come out here again soon."

Joseph finally pulled in the fish. Joshua had been right. This fish was well over a foot and a half long.

All of a sudden Joshua yelled out, "Father, I think I have one, too! It's pulling really hard on my line. I can tell it's a big one."

Starting to reel in the line, he got more and more excited. Careful not to lose his catch, he reeled it in more gently. Finally it emerged from the water, and Joshua's face dropped, and then he had to laugh.

"Father, look at my catch!"

Joseph had already seen what his son had caught and was quietly laughing, though he tried not to. Joshua had caught an old burlap bag, which when he emptied it on shore was full of empty soda cans.

Joshua, realizing how ridiculous he must appear, looked at his father and just laughed. "Well, Father, I can at least bring the cans to the store and get the deposit. Twenty cans. That's one dollar. Not bad for my first fishing trip. I already made a profit."

Joseph laughed, happy that his son could see humor in his disappointment.

It was hard to tell who was the most excited over the size of their catch. Neither could wait to get home to show Miriam. As they neared the house, they spotted her sitting on the porch reading a book.

"Mother, mother!" Joshua called out. "Look what father caught."

Miriam jumped up in shock at seeing the huge fish. She had no idea they would ever catch a fish that size so close to the village.

"I think they call it a trout, Mother. I heard the boys talking about it yesterday," Joshua continued.

Joseph did not have the heart to hand it to his wife to clean and prepare, even though she made a move to take it from him.

"I'll get it ready, dear, and I know you can do a much better job cooking it than I could. So, if you and Joshua don't mind preparing the fire . . ."

"Shall we cook it like in the old days, over an open fire, Joseph?"

"That would be wonderful. It's a perfect size for that."

Joshua ran to the back of the yard to get the wood while his father washed the fish and his mother brought a large platter and utensils and dishes to prepare the little picnic table. It is hard to imagine the joy and excitement of that little family over such a simple experience. For people who have little, the simplest surprise fills their hearts with gladness. So often for people who have much, even the most awesome experiences fail to excite them.

That afternoon and evening was a time in their lives they would not soon forget.

T HAT NIGHT WHEN JOSHUA WENT TO BED, HE FELT
a real need to talk to his "Father in heaven." He was
getting used to treating him as a real part of his life. Ever
since his mother had reminded him that his Father in heaven
whom he was always talking about had given him his special
gifts, which he would need as he got older, Joshua felt an
even greater closeness to him and felt he could ask him personally now when he had a question or when something was
bothering him. What was bothering him this time was how
he knew there was a big fish where he told Joseph to cast his
fishing line.

Kneeling at his bedside, he just spoke his prayers as if
he were in a conversation with someone standing there:
"Father, when I told my father to cast his fishing line to his
left, I knew there was a fish there and a big one. How did I
know that, Father? Things like this happen to me a lot, and
it makes me feel strange. Help me to understand, Father."

Joshua waited and listened for an answer. Nothing.

"Father, why don't you answer me? I need to know."

Still nothing. Joshua was disappointed.

Lying down and resting his head on his pillow, he began to doze off. A quiet thought drifted across his sleepy mind, "Because our thoughts are one."

But Joshua was too sleepy for it to make an impression. Soon he was sound asleep.

"That sure was a big fish," Joseph said to Joshua as they were eating breakfast. "How did you know that fish would be there?"

"I guess because that's where it jumped out of the water the day before. It was around there someplace."

Joseph was still not convinced. It just didn't make sense that a fish would stay in the same place in the middle of a lake. But he said nothing more about it.

"Have a good day at school, Son," he said as Joshua kissed him and his mother and picked up his books to leave.

"Don't work too hard, Abba. I'll help you when I come home. I love you both. Bye."

"Good-bye, Son," his mother called out as he jumped off the front steps and started up the street.

"That boy is so confusing sometimes, Miriam. I knew he had something to do with that water and wine incident a while back. And now this fish. It's uncanny."

"He's a very special boy, dear. We always knew that. How special, I don't even know. And he always keeps saying 'My Father in heaven.' When I ask him what he means when he says that, he tells me that he doesn't know. He just says it because he feels very close to Yahweh. He is such a lovable child. Thank God he is so good."

"I still worry about him, Miriam. Having a child like that is such a responsibility."

"I know, Joseph. I worry, too. The words of that priest

Simeon keep haunting me. I can never forget them. 'This child is destined for the fall and rise of many in Israel, and for a sign that shall be contradicted. And your own soul a sword shall pierce, that the thoughts of many hearts may be revealed.' What does it all mean?"

"We have to trust God, Miriam. Only he knows what the future will bring. We can't worry. It does no good, and God knows what he is doing. His plans will not be frustrated. And my own plan for today is that I have to work up at the mill, dear. It's only until two o'clock. I'll be back after that and finish up some work in the yard. Oh, I almost forgot. There is a good movie playing in the city. The name of it is, 'Oh, God!' It's a simple movie, but it should be fun. Would you like to go? It will be a surprise for Joshua."

"That would be a nice change. We've been working hard, and I need a break. We'll have to take an early bus so we can be home at a reasonable time. I could have supper ready early. I'll make a pizza."

"Good. I'll get my work done fast so I can be ready. I'm curious as to what Joshua's reaction will be to the movie. He seems to have his own ideas about God."

As Joseph started to leave for work, Miriam gave him the lunch she had prepared. Joseph kissed her tenderly and left, almost breaking his leg as he tried to imitate Joshua by jumping down the front steps. Miriam could not help laughing. He looked so funny.

"I guess I'm not a kid anymore. Bye, dear!"

Bye, Joseph. I'll miss you."

Alone for a few quiet hours, Miriam withdrew to the special room Joseph had refurbished for her. There she retired to paint, and knit, and pray. Since her childhood, like Joshua, she had been powerfully drawn to intimacy with the Lord. Her prayers were mostly psalms, and personal prayers her mother had taught her as a child. Though of late, her prayers were centering more and more on her child, though he was hardly a child any longer. Even though she knew he was special to God, as a mother she still worried. All she saw was his goodness and innocence and his childlike simplicity, traits that she knew would make him vulnerable to the schemes of others.

What she did not see developing beneath the surface of Joshua's simplicity was his growing awareness of evil in the world. His instincts and slowly emerging sensing of evil and dishonesty in others was cultivating in him the wariness of a fox. He was learning fast not to share too much with others.

He was also beginning to see that human friendships could be as shifty as the wind, never the same and so often fickle, loyal one day and then hurtful for no apparent reason. He was inclined to be open in sharing with his friends. He wondered why they could not be open and honest like he was. Noticing this difference again made him aware that he was different.

An incident happened in school that day that had a disturbing effect on Joshua. A girl named Ruth in Joshua's class had a crush on Joshua. She knew that Joshua and Marguerite were good friends, which made her extremely jealous. Not knowing how to get Joshua's attention, she told one of Joshua's friends, Marty, who liked Ruth, that Joshua was trying to steal her away from him. On the way into class Marty walked past Joshua and poked him with his elbow as he went by. Joshua turned and Marty just ignored him. Joshua could tell he was upset about something, but could not imagine what it could be.

At the noon lunch break Marty came over to Joshua, pushed him in the chest with his open hand, and in an angry tone warned him to keep away from his friend Ruth. Joshua was completely baffled and merely muttered, "Marty, I don't know what you're talking about."

"You know what I mean. Keep away from her."

"Marty," Joshua continued half laughing, "you're not making sense. I don't know what you mean."

Joshua laughing at him made Marty furious. He swung and hit Joshua in the face, which caused a lot of students to gather, hoping there would be a fight.

Joshua stepped back, realizing how upset his friend was. When Marty went to hit him again, Joshua quickly raised his opened left hand and blocked Marty's punch. Marty continued with a left hook, but Joshua blocked that one, too. Every time Marty swung, Joshua blocked it.

"I am not going to fight with you, Marty. You're my friend and I will never strike you, so you might as well stop trying to get me to fight. It's stupid."

Finally Marty gave up and, frustrated, merely warned Joshua once more, "Well, keep away from Ruth." Then he walked off to go home for lunch.

Joshua walked away mystified.

Marguerite came running toward Joshua. Someone had told her and a group of girls that there was going to be a fight, and that one of the boys fighting was Joshua.

"Joshua, what happened?" she cried out to him, concerned.

"Oh, nothing. Just a misunderstanding, I guess. I think people sometimes say things about others that are not true. Someone must have said something to my friend Marty and got him all upset. But it's all over now."

"Are you all right?"

"Yes, I wasn't going to fight with him."

"Why is your face all red?"

"He got me by surprise," Joshua said, laughing, "but after

that I was faster than he was, so I blocked him each time he tried to punch me."

"I thought he was your friend."

"He's still my friend. Someone must have said something to him that was not true. He'll get over it."

"Joshua, don't you ever get mad at anybody?

"Not with a friend. If I can understand I don't get mad. When someone is mean and really tries to hurt someone, I can become angry."

"Do you go home for lunch or do you eat lunch here?" Marguerite asked him.

"I just eat a sandwich, which I bring with me, and then I like to see my friends, or take a walk and think. I like to think."

"You're amazing, Joshua. You're different, aren't you?"

Joshua was quiet for a moment. There was that word again, "different."

"Do you think I'm different?"

"Yes, but in a nice way. You are someone really special. I don't know how to say it. But you're someone everyone likes to be near. You make everyone feel good, like peaceful. I don't know how to say what I mean."

She continued, "Well, I have to go home for lunch. I am glad nothing serious happened between you and Marty. I'll see you later."

"Bye, Marguerite."

When afternoon classes were over and he arrived at home, the surprise of going to the movies took away all the gloom. He was thrilled, especially when his mother told him the name of the movie.

"Mother, that should be fun. I heard it was very funny. I can't wait to see it."

"Your father mentioned it, and we thought it would be a good idea since we have all been working so hard."

Joseph entered and saw Joshua's thrill over the prospect of going to the movies.

"You'll have to get ready, Son. If we are going to catch the bus to the city and see the early movie, we'll have to rush."

Joshua was so excited he got ready in no time at all and ran down the stairs to eat his supper, which was probably the shortest suppertime they had ever had. Finishing their pizza and salad, they were out to meet the bus in fifteen minutes flat. Like children at Christmas, they were caught up in the excitement of something so simple as going to a movie, one that probably everyone else in the village had already seen.

During the movie what was most entertaining for Miriam and Joseph was watching their son laugh so loud and so often whenever George Burns, playing God, said something Joshua thought was clever. They could not imagine what it was that seemed so hilarious to him. He laughed the hardest when God made it rain inside the car while the sun was shining outside.

On the way home after the movie, both his parents were intensely curious as to what he had found so funny. Did he think God was that way?

"No, my Father in heaven is more subtle than that, but I found the things that happened in the movie really funny. My friends call that kind of funny stuff slapstick, but I enjoy it and it takes my mind off serious things and makes me laugh."

The movie did distract him from the unpleasantness earlier in the day.

"Did you enjoy the movie, Father?"

"Yes, I did, Son. But I have to admit, it was more fun watching you all during the movie and how much you enjoyed it. You were quite an entertaining sideshow."

Miriam laughed. "You really enjoy life, don't you, Son?"

"Yes, I do, Mother, especially waking up in the morning to each new day. I like to open the window and smell the fresh air and look into the yard and see the bright, shiny sun lighting up the trees and shrubs and pretty plants, and watch the birds flying so gracefully from tree to tree, singing happy songs."

Joseph fell asleep long before the bus reached the village, so Joshua and his mother spoke softly so they would not wake him. It was good for him to sleep; he needed his rest.

"You worry a lot about Father, don't you, Mother? I can tell. I watch your eyes and your face. When you look at him sometimes, I notice you look sad."

"Yes, Son, I do worry about him. Sometimes I don't think he's well, though the doctors never find anything wrong. I wish he would rest more and not work so hard. I'd worry a lot less. I try to cook healthy meals for him, hoping they will be healing."

"I know you worry, Mother. I worry about him, too. That's why sometimes I think he should have something at supper to build up his strength after he has had a hard day at work."

"I suspected that is what had happened, Joshua; the time when I asked you to pour water in our glasses. Son, your Father in heaven has given you special abilities for good reason. But I hope you don't do things like that outside. You have those gifts to help people and not for play, or to entertain people. So use those gifts wisely. And don't discuss them with anyone, not even your best friends, because friends may not always be friends, and whatever you share with them, they may one day use to hurt you."

"Mother, I wish I could learn to cook. Someday I may have to cook for myself, and I want to be able to cook the nice things you make, the ones I like. I mean, you know what I mean, everything you cook I like, but some I like special."

Miriam laughed at Joshua's getting trapped in his words, especially since he was usually so precise.

"I like the soup you made last week, the 'healthy' soup you called it."

"That's an easy soup to make. I just used all my leftover vegetables. I had some broccoli, and cauliflower, and onion and garlic, and mushrooms, and celery and green beans, and a lot of cabbage, and diced tomatoes, and a lot of Creole seasoning. I put it all in chicken broth and let it boil for three quarters of an hour at medium heat. Then I put in a half cup of marinara sauce I had saved from a previous dinner."

"That was delicious, Mother. I think I can remember that recipe. Can I try to make it next time?"

"Yes, but you'll have to come home right after school so we will have time to cut up the vegetables and get everything ready."

"When are you going to make it again?"

"Probably next week."

"I can't wait. That will be the first meal that I cooked all by myself."

"Joshua, you are so funny. I cannot get over how much you enjoy life and make such simple things an adventure. Don't ever lose your sense of wonder and your ability to find joy in simple things."

"Things are not always happy, Mother, but I try to think

about the happy things. I don't like thinking about the painful things. They hurt too much and make you angry. I don't like being angry. I try to understand why people do hurtful things, and I think it's because they're not happy. Then I don't get angry at them."

The bus finally arrived at Shadybrook.

Joshua playfully nudged his father. "Father, are you going to come home with us?"

Joseph woke up from a deep sleep. "We're home already?"

"That was a fun night, Abba. Thank you," Joshua said as they entered the house and he started upstairs to bed.

Kneeling at his bedside, he could see the stars through his window. They looked like lights from another world. He held his arms out as if reaching for that world as he talked to his "Father in heaven."

"Father, today was a difficult day. One of my friends was mad at me for something. I don't know what it's about. I hope he's over whatever it was. I will treat him tomorrow as if nothing happened, and hope that it's past. And it was fun going out to the movies tonight with my parents. I love them very much, Father. But, I worry about my father. I feel he's not well. I don't know why I worry. I do trust you, Father, but I don't understand your plans for my father, and I think that's what makes me worry. Please help him, Father, and give him strength and healing. I love you, Father. Good night. And bless that boy who is angry at me."

THE SUN POURED IN THROUGH JOSHUA'S WINDOW, and with the first rays of light came Joshua's friend, the cardinal, pecking at the window. Joshua had put a tray of seed on the windowsill, which attracted not only the cardinal but other birds as well. This morning an indigo bunting was perched on the edge of the feeder, paying no attention to the cardinal. As Joshua reached outside the open window, the bunting flew away, but the cardinal hopped onto his wrist and ate the birdseed from his hand, feeling comfortable and secure with his new friend. Joshua looked forward to this each morning.

After a few minutes, the indigo bunting flew back to the feeder and pecked at the seed, then, watching the cardinal, it too hopped onto Joshua's hand and started to eat the seed. The cardinal was not at all pleased and moved up on Joshua's arm and stayed there watching until the other bird flew away. Then Joshua brought the cardinal inside and chatted with it, wondering if it understood what he was saying.

"Joshua, I hope you're getting ready for school. You don't want to be late," his mother called up to him.

"I'll be down in a few minutes, Mother. I'm just saying hello to my friend. I think I have a new one. It is very pretty."

Joshua let the bird fly out the window and, after taking his shower, he rushed downstairs.

"I want to get to school early. I have to meet my friend, Jimmy. His father, who's a wood-carver, made something for me, and I can't wait to see what it is."

"Don't rush your breakfast, Joshua. You should be relaxed when you eat so you can digest your food. It's not good to rush your meals."

Joseph did not talk much at breakfast. It usually took him a while to wake up, so he just quietly ate and listened to the two of them talk. It was the same almost every morning; Joshua rushing and his mother trying to slow him down. It was better if he kept out of it anyway.

After Joshua finished his breakfast, Joseph did say something as his son kissed him on the cheek.

"Be careful, Son! And pick your friends wisely! They are not all as innocent as you are."

"Yes, Abba. I try to have good friends. Most of them are. Some have problems. But I'm careful. I'll be home right after school, Mother," he said as he kissed her and ran out the door, letting it slam behind him.

His friend Jimmy was waiting for him, all excited about giving him the present his father had carved for him.

"Joshua, wait till you see it. It is beautiful," he said as he held the package out to Joshua.

"What is it, Jimmy?"

"It's a surprise. You have to open it."

Joshua excitedly opened the gift, which was wrapped in ordinary brown paper, probably a cut-up grocery bag.

When he opened it, he was thrilled.

"Jimmy, this is the greatest gift I ever had," he said as he admired the replica of an ancient fishing boat. "This brings back so many memories."

"So many memories? Memories of what, Joshua?"

"I don't know, just memories that float around in my mind, of things that cross my mind a lot when I'm asleep. This is so beautiful, Jimmy. I want to thank your father for his kindness."

"He loves to carve. I could tell he was so happy as he was carving this for you. He is so glad you are my friend. He thinks you are very special. My father prays a lot, and he told me I was blessed to have a friend like you. I always knew that, but it meant a lot to hear my father say it."

"Thank you, Jimmy. And I am blessed to have a friend like you. I can trust you."

The two boys walked into school together just as the bell rang.

As soon as class started and the Pledge of Allegiance was said, the teacher announced that a war had just started. A loud sucking of air crossed the room as the children were startled. As Joshua had not listened to the radio before coming to school that day, he was as shocked as the others in his class.

In his innocent surprise he put up his hand, and when the teacher looked at him, he burst out the question, "Why do people kill one another? They are all God's children. Don't they know it's evil to kill God's children?"

Stunned at the innocence of the question, the teacher did not know how to reply, so she said nothing. The children as well were shocked at Joshua's question. They turned and looked at him. Joshua could not understand why everybody was acting so strangely. Then he remembered his mother once telling him that teachers may not know how to reply to the serious questions he might ask, so he did not press the issue, but it still troubled him that people could be ordered by leaders to go out and kill other people. Now, he couldn't wait to go home and pour his heart out to his mother, and this time to his father, too. He was restless through all his classes as he struggled to try to understand why people needed to kill one another in order to solve problems. He did not understand how it could make sense.

When the class ended, Miss Axeman called Joshua aside and quietly said to him that the kind of question he asked should not be asked in school. "We are not supposed to talk about God in school."

"Why can't we talk about God in school?" he asked with a puzzled look.

"Because this is a democracy and everyone is free."

"Isn't that all the more reason why we should be free to talk about God?"

"Joshua, I feel the way you do, but it is against the law. So, please don't ask any more questions like that in class."

"I don't understand. My Father in heaven gave us freedom, but we are not free to talk about him, as if he is only make-believe, and not real. This is his world, and we are his children."

"It might hurt somebody's feelings if we talk about God. It violates their rights."

"What about my feelings when I am told I cannot talk about God? What about my rights to express what I believe?"

"Oh, Joshua, what am I going to do with you? You are such a lovable, precocious child, and I love you dearly, but you are so different, so wonderfully different, I don't know what to say to you sometimes."

There was that word again, "so different." "I am different," he thought. "Even my teacher whom I love thinks I'm different. Why do people keep saying that?"

"Joshua, people have been fighting and killing all through history. It seems we never learn to solve problems in a peaceful way, and then some leaders feel they are powerful enough to do what they want and get away with it. So, it never ends. Now, my dear young Joshua, don't trouble your dear heart with such heavy problems. You will have to face them soon enough. Enjoy being a happy boy while you are still young. Your happy years will fly by so fast."

Joshua thanked her for taking the time to talk to him, but his mind was still not at rest.

Outside the school afterward, two of his friends asked him why he was so upset in class when the teacher talked about the war. He tried to explain himself all over again, but his friends could not understand why it bothered him. "There are wars on television all the time. There have always been wars. They're exciting. I'm going to become a soldier when I'm eighteen," Johnny said.

"I don't see them as exciting. I think they are terrible. My Father creates people with love and then they kill each other. It is evil," Joshua said. "My father creates people to care for each other, and they think it is smart to kill each other. It does not make sense. Why can't people talk so they can understand? Animals fight because they can't think. People are part angel and they fight like animals."

Joshua realized that even in this he was different, and

knew that his friends could not understand. So he changed the subject. "I prayed for your mother, Johnny. I know she will be get better."

"How did you know about my mother?"

"When is she coming home from the hospital?"

"I don't know. My father is going to take me to see her tonight."

The boys parted ways, and Joshua could not wait to get home so he could share his problem with his parents. He passed Marguerite on the way and waved to her from across the street, but didn't stop to talk.

As he approached the house, his father was weeding the garden.

"Need some help, Abba?"

"That would be nice, Son. I'm a little tired, and it will give me a chance to rest. How was school?"

"It was okay."

"Just okay? You usually sound happy about school."

"Some things I don't understand."

"Like what, Joshua?"

"The teacher said that we are at war, and I asked why people have to fight, because God made us to care for one another, and war is evil. She said we could not discuss God in class, and she looked nervous, and then went on to teach the class. After class she took me aside and explained to me that it is not allowed to talk about God in school, that it might offend people who do not believe in God. Father, I don't understand that and I was offended that I was not free to talk about God. I would like to talk to you and Mother about it later."

"That would be fine, Son. Why don't you change your clothes and do a little weeding, then we can get ready for supper, and we can discuss it then."

Joshua liked to work in the garden. His favorite flowers were the simple poppies that grew so profusely and made the yard look so cheerful. After weeding, he moved back and sat on the grass and stared at the garden for the longest time, lost in thought. He loved to drink in the beauty of all the colors. They made him feel peaceful and think about his Father in heaven's love for us.

"Thank you, Father, for the beautiful flowers. You created them just to make us happy, and lift our spirits when we are hurting. I am hurting today, Father. It is sad that we cannot talk about you in school. I don't like the way people treat you, Father, especially since you are so good to them. Why do I feel hurt, Father, when I know you feel hurt? And when someone says something about you that is not right, why do I always take your side and try to explain you? Why am I so different? I think so much like you think, and I don't thnk my friends are like that. Father, I am so glad we are close. I love you, Father."

When Joshua finished his daydreaming, he looked up and saw his mother standing on the porch smiling down at him.

"What were you dreaming about, Son? You were deep in thought."

"I was thanking my Father in heaven for the beautiful flowers."

"Are you coming inside? It's almost time for supper."

"Mother, I have to talk to you and Father. I have something troubling me."

"After you go up and wash, come down and we can talk at dinner." Joshua jumped up and went to his room to wash. As soon as they sat down for supper, Miriam opened the conversation.

"Now, Son, what is it that you wanted to share with us?"

"The teacher told us the country is at war. I put my hand up and said we are all God's children, and asked 'Don't they know it is evil to kill God's children?' I think she was shocked and didn't say anything. After class, she took me aside and told me that we are not allowed to talk about God in school because this is a democracy and we are all free to believe what we choose. I told her that was more reason why we should feel free to talk about God. He is *real*. He's not *make-believe*. Then she said it was against the law becasue talking about God might offend someone who does not believe in God. I told her then that the law restricts my freedom to speak and express what *I* think? And I cannot understand why anyone should be offended if someone expresses what they think, even if it is about God. The teacher was nice, but I could tell she was exasperated with me, like you get exasperated with me when I get difficult."

His parents looked at each other and laughed. Joshua laughed, too, knowing that he could be difficult at times, not because he was nasty but because he was so persistent, especially when he was trying to figure out something that was difficult to understand.

"Son, we live in a new kind of society," Joseph said. "It is a young society, and it is still trying to understand itself. One of the important issues in a society like this is for people to have respect for each other. It is an ideal, and a noble ideal. But you are right; it is possible, in trying to protect one person's rights, they may violate another person's right to freedom, like what you experienced today."

"So, Father, I will continue to ask questions that I think are important. I want to understand, and I have a right to ask questions even if someone doesn't like the questions I ask."

"It's your right, Joshua, and even though we smile at

your persistence, we both admire you very much. You are very bright for your age, and we both know that you can handle this problem. But, be patient with the teacher, and be respectful, and always be willing to listen."

"Thank you both. I feel better now. Even my supper tastes better."

"Joshua, I have a little surprise in the yard. I was able to get some special lumber at work today, and you can help me make our surprise after supper."

"I can't wait. What is it, Abba?"

"It's a surprise. That's all I'm going to say."

Joshua couldn't wait until he finished supper so he could go out into the yard and see the surprise. "What is it going to be, Abba, this pile of lumber?"

"Three guesses."

"A picnic table?"

"No."

"A shed where I can go on rainy days and think, and invite my friends for parties?"

"No."

"A fishing boat?" he said in an excited voice.

"Yes, so the next time we go fishing, we won't have to traipse through all that water."

"Abba, can we make two of them? One for us, and one for my friends? Because they won't all fit in one boat."

"Well, let's make one first and see how it turns out. Then if we do a good job, we can start on another one."

"This is going to be fun," Joshua said as they both got their tools and other materials together.

"We'll have to cut some pieces of wood and soak them in water for a day or two, to bend them into the shape we need. We want the boat to have some nice curves as well as be sturdy."

The two started to work. Joshua mostly watched, never taking his eyes off his father to make sure he was learning everything.

"Father, you've already started work on the boat. It's a clever idea to make the front of the boat first, shaped like an arrow on the top down to the bottom, with the groove already cut, so all you have to do is insert the slats in place and nail them."

"Son, I am going to screw them in place. They will hold better. But, before we drive the screws I am going to glue the wood, and then screw the boards into the bow. Here, hold this board in place while I put in one of the screws. Then you can do the next one."

Starting with the bottom of the boat, each board as it was put in place overlapped the board beneath it. The boards were tapered at the bottom to look almost flush with the board beneath. Each board was glued where it overlapped the lower one.

"Father, this is going to be a big boat. These boards are twelve feet long."

"It will be comfortable, because I would like to take your mother with us sometimes, and if the boat is big and comfortable, she'll be more likely to come with us."

"You always think of Mother, don't you?"

"She's all I have, Son, and her whole life is dedicated to you and me. She does everything for us, so I like to show her how much I appreciate all that she does. So, yes, Joshua, I do always think of her, and how I can make her life a little easier."

"Father, this motorized screwdriver is heavy. I have to hold it with two hands."

"Take your time, Joshua. I'll hold the board; just take

your time. The screw is already partially in place. So just drive it in the rest of the way."

"There. How is that, Father?"

"Very good, Son."

Finishing the one side of the boat, Joseph told Joshua they now had to put the wood in water so it could be bent more easily. So, putting the section they had just finished in a trough that Joseph used for mixing cement, they filled it with water and left it to soak overnight.

"Now, if you come right home from school tomorrow we can get an early start, and get a good part of the boat finished. Since I don't have to go to work tomorrow, I will work with the wood while you are in school, so I'll be ready for you to help me as soon as you come home."

"I can't wait, Father. It's going to be a beautiful boat."

Joshua was all excited when he went inside and told his mother what they had already done, and how he even helped his father put the boards together.

"I was watching you through the window. That's going to be a big boat."

"That's so you will feel comfortable coming with us when we go fishing or for a ride."

"We'll see. Well, you'd better get ready for bed."

As Joshua knelt at his bedside, his conversation with his Father in heaven was full of excitement as he told his Father how much fun it was to work on the boat, and that he couldn't wait until it was finished.

And, jumping into bed, he ended his prayer, "It is so much fun being in this beautiful world you created. Thank you, Father. Bless those people who suffer from want and loneliness and tragedy. Let them know you love them, too, Father. Life cannot be easy for them."

THE NEXT DAY, MISS AXEMAN KEPT LOOKING AT Joshua during class. She could see there was something unusual about this gentle, thoughtful boy, who was so much like the others, yet so deep for his age. Joshua noticed how she looked at him. He could tell she liked him and felt badly that she could not answer his question in class.

Though it had been her custom previously to discuss current events with each of her classes, she would be more careful from now on so as not to give her precocious student any openings. He saw things in a way that would never cross other students' minds, and his unusual questions could make a teacher uncomfortable. Not that it would bother the students, but some parent might become upset if a student were to say there was a discussion about God in school.

Miss Axeman thought it silly that anyone should be offended by a student asking a question about God in class, but, realizing that we live in times when society is sensitive about everyone's rights, she thought it best to be careful.

Joshua's concentration, however, was more on the boat he and his father were making than on his class subjects, and he could not wait until recess so he could run home and help his father with it. Between classes he told his friends what he and his father were doing, and they were thrilled. One of the boys told Joshua his uncle owned the property where the pond was located. This uncle told his nephew that he and his friends could play there if they were careful. The boy also told his uncle that Joshua's father might make a boat if they could use the pond, and he smiled and said it was okay. So, now that they had permission to use the property, it was literally clear sailing.

When Joshua arrived at home, Joseph had already made progress on the boat. He had constructed a mechanism for bending the wood to form the front of the boat. This would hold the wood in shape for a few days until it dried. After having done that earlier in the day, Joseph cut slats for the sides and set them aside until they were ready to put them in place.

There was not very much that Joshua could do, but Joseph taught him how to use the various saws and planes, and how to be precise when sawing wood. It was important that everything be done neatly and with precision. Joshua was curious as to how his father had bent the wood. It took a while for him to explain how he put everything together and how he was able to bend the wood easily. It was not too difficult as the wood was less than half an inch thick.

The two of them spent the next couple of hours cutting the wood for the bottom and back of the boat, and for the seats. Joshua let out a deep sigh of relief after all the hard work. His father laughed that he was so tired after working for only two hours.

"Hard work, Joshua, eh?" his father said with a smile.

"I know, Father, and you worked all day. It was fun working with you. You're my best friend. I love you, Abba."

"I love you, too, Son."

It was almost time for supper.

Washing up before coming to the supper table, Joshua could smell what his mother had prepared. He remembered it was the meal his mother had promised to teach him how to make. Tucking in his shirt as he entered the kitchen, he reminded Miriam of her promise.

"Joshua, I'm sorry. I forgot all about it. I still have some ingredients on the counter that I didn't use in preparing supper. I'll show you after supper."

"Good, Mother. I want to learn how to cook, so when I get older I can do my own cooking. And what you cook is so good."

"Thank you, Son."

"Father, I can't wait until we finish our boat, so we can take Mother for a ride. You'll come with us, Mother, won't you?"

"We'll see. I never rode in a boat before. The men always used them for fishing, and for their work."

"Mother, you have to come. It will be a lot of fun. And maybe you can even go fishing with us."

"If you mean putting bait on the hooks, I don't think so, Joshua."

"Well, you don't have to bait the hooks. Father and I can do that. Just come to be with us. It won't be as much fun without you."

Then looking at her husband, Miriam asked him, "Joseph, someone must own that property. I hope you got permission from the owner to put a boat on his lake and go fishing there."

"My dear, I already thought of that. I met the man at the lumberyard and talked to him about it. He is an old man and lives way down at the other end of the lake. He said he would be happy to let us use it. He told me he walks through the village occasionally and sees Joshua frequently. He likes him, and said he is such a happy boy. Just watching him makes him smile. There is something different about that boy, he keeps telling me.

"All the other kids ignore him because he is just another old man, but Joshua always makes him happy, just by saying hello and helping him cross the street. He thinks Joshua is very special. I thanked him for his kind words, and when he told me where he lives, I offered to do his shopping for him if he'd let me know what he needs from the store. He was happy about that."

"Father, I can do that for you. I know where that man lives, in a little shack down by the lake."

"We'll see, Son."

With supper over, Miriam called Joshua over to the counter and told him the recipe for the soup she had made. It was very simple.

"Now, Joshua, you can help me. Cut up the broccoli stalks in thin slices, and put them aside. Now cut up the cauliflower into smaller pieces, then slice the mushrooms, and the green beans, and the celery, and the carrots, and that green pepper from your father's garden, and cut up the rest of that head of cabbage, and one of those onions, and put it all to one side. Take those five tomatoes out of that basket, cut them into small pieces, and put them and the vegetables in this big four-quart pan.

"In the refrigerator is a container of chicken broth I made yesterday. Put half of that broth in the pan, and add a cup of water. Put in a teaspoon of salt and a tablespoon of Creole seasoning. In the refrigerator is a jar of marinara sauce I made. Put a cup of that sauce on top of the vegetables.

"Now turn on the burner to medium heat, cover the pan, and put it on the burner. Turn on the timer so it can alert you when the time is up. Let it cook for three quarters of an hour, then taste it and see if you like it. Now, Joshua, I am sure you have homework to do, so why don't you go upstairs and do what you have to do. When you hear the timer, you can come back down and finish your cooking."

"Mother, that was fun. I hope it turns out all right and tastes like yours."

"I'm sure it will."

During all this time, Joseph tried to read his newspaper, but could not resist watching the cooking lesson and enjoyed the show.

"Father," Joshua said as he walked past his father, now engrossed in his newspaper, "remember you promised to teach me how to make sausage like the ones we had last week?"

"I was just thinking of it, Joshua, as I was watching your mother teaching you how to cook that soup. I will teach you tomorrow evening, after we do some more work on our boat."

"Joshua!" His mother called up to him when he did not respond to the timer on the stove. "The timer went off. You didn't fall asleep, did you?"

Joshua came running down the stairs.

"It didn't burn, did it?"

"No, but I think you had better stir it to mix it all up. You might want to cook it a little more. Taste it and see if you like it."

"Mother, it tastes just like yours."

"I wonder why."

"You're funny."

"Did you finish your homework?"

"Well, sort of. I got most of it done, then I fell asleep. I'll finish it when I go back upstairs. I'm glad you heard the timer go off."

"I have a little suggestion, since you made quite a bit of soup. Take half of it and put it in the blender and puree it, and put a level teaspoon of sugar in it."

After doing this, he tasted it. "Mother, I like it this way. It tastes a lot better like this."

Taking the plastic containers that were lying off to the side, he filled them and put them in the freezer.

"Now I have cooked my own meal. Can we have it for supper tomorrow, Mother?"

"We had it tonight. Why not wait until the next night."

"Okay. I can't wait."

That night was a frightful experience for Joshua. Terrible dreams disturbed his sleep all through the night. When he woke up, it was raining outside. The birds did not show up. An unusual depression filled his heart and he could not shake it. His usual happy spirit had departed.

His mother was the first to notice the change in her son as soon as he came down the stairs. His quick step was gone. Each step was slow and deliberate. His whole demeanor had changed from his exuberant mood from just a few hours ago.

"Joshua, what's the matter? You don't seem like your happy self this morning. What's troubling you, Son?"

"Mother, something terrible has happened to one of my friends. Jimmy is in terrible trouble."

"How do you know that, Son?"

"I just know, Mother. I always know when something is going to happen to someone, especially if the person is a friend."

"Did you have a bad dream?"

"Mother, it was not a dream. It came to me during my sleep, but it was not a dream. Even when I am awake I know these things. It is very painful for me, Mother. I have to go and see my friend Jimmy. He is such a good boy. I hope he'll be all right. I will have to talk to my Father in heaven."

At that point Joseph came into the kitchen.

"What's the trouble? Are you all right, Joshua?"

"He's had a bad dream, Joseph, and it is very upsetting for him. He'll be all right."

"Mother, it was not a dream. I just know that something has happened to my friend, and I have to go and see him before school starts."

"Joshua, you have to eat first."

"Mother, I can't eat. I have no appetite. Please believe me. I have to go and help Jimmy."

As he walked to the door, his mother followed him, giving him the bag lunch she had made for him.

"Take this, Son. You may not feel like eating now, but at lunchtime you will be hungry."

Reluctantly, his parents let him go to school without eating breakfast. Miriam stood at the doorway and watched her troubled son walk up the street. So young a boy to have such deep feelings, she was thinking. Simeon's words crossed her mind: "This child is destined . . . Your own soul a sword shall pierce." Tears welled up in her eyes as Joseph walked up behind her and put his arms around her, trying to comfort her.

It is hard for fathers to understand the bond between mother and children. This child was even more difficult to understand. There were angels involved in his life from the start, which made Joseph realize that God had an intimate role in this child's life. The boy was a source of wonderful joy, but there were times when his life occasioned great pain. The boy was different, even though he tried so hard to be like everyone else.

"Oh, Joseph, I worry so much about that boy. His whole life is surrounded with mystery. At times I think I understand him, then there are times when he is so far away, and as he gets older he seems to grow farther away, and it becomes more and more difficult to understand what is happening inside him.

"He is often so happy and so lighthearted, then there are times . . . and I can see it in his eyes, a sadness, a pain, as if he is carrying the weight of the world on his heart. And I feel every pain he does. I am finally beginning to understand the words of that old man, Simeon."

"Miriam, Miriam, my dear, I know I will never be able to understand. I have never been able to understand, right from the beginning. All I know is that there is a mystery to our lives. The boy is different. We are all different. I am beginning to realize this more and more each day.

"Although I will never be able to comprehend what God has planned for Joshua, I know he is destined for something that will affect the lives of all of us. I also share in some small way in the pain that you feel over the mystery to which God has entrusted us."

"Oh, Joseph, you have been so good, so compassionate and kind. I know it has never been easy for you. I watch you sometimes and I know life is not easy for you. I know you are not well, and my heart aches for you. I know Joshua is special to you, too. When you hear him talking about his 'Father in heaven,' can you understand what he is talking about? I asked him and he tries to tell me, but I don't think he understands himself."

"I've overheard him telling you about his 'Father in

heaven.' Even though he may not understand it yet, I think I understand what he is saying. He is really saying, without realizing the implications, that Yahweh is his Father. The two of them must communicate, even though Joshua doesn't even understand fully what it is all about. I think his Father in heaven must have shared something with him last night that upset him deeply. I can understand why he could not eat his breakfast. It will be interesting to hear what he has to tell us when he comes home from school this afternoon. Why don't we just pray for him, and ask his Father in heaven to hold him close to himself, and keep him from harm."

Walking into the kitchen, they sat down across from each other at the table and, holding hands, prayed from deep in their hearts for this blessed child whom neither of them could understand, but whose life would always be a mystery mixed with extraordinary joy and extraordinary pain.

In the meantime, Joshua went looking for his friend Jimmy. He asked everyone he saw if they had seen him. No one had seen him. He was usually at school early, waiting for Joshua and some of his other friends, but this morning he was nowhere to be found. Joshua walked all over and finally found him in an empty lot, sitting on the trunk of a fallen tree.

"Jimmy, Jimmy, what happened to you? Are you all right?"

The boy looked up, surprised to see Joshua. He looked horrible. His eyes had dark circles. He was shaking and unsteady and unable to talk right.

Joshua went over to him, sat down on the log next to him, and hugged him hard.

"Jimmy, Jimmy, my dear friend. What is it that is hurting you so much that you have to do this to yourself?"

Joshua knew he had become addicted to a powerful and dangerous drug.

Moved that Joshua should know so much and that he cared, the boy started to cry. Putting his face on Joshua's shoulder, he cried his heart out as Joshua continued to hug him.

"Joshua, I am so miserable. It is terrible at home. My mother and father fight all the time and say terrible things to each other. I can't sleep nights and I don't feel like eating anymore. I take this stuff to ease my pain, but it really doesn't help. It makes things even more of a hell. I want to die."

"Jimmy, you don't have to die to escape this pain. I am your friend and I will help you. I feel your pain, and I can help you. Trust me. I will talk to my Father in heaven. He always listens to me and grants what I ask him."

As Joshua moved to stand up, he lifted Jimmy up with him and looked deeply into his eyes. Although Jimmy did not want to look at him, he could not resist. He looked into Joshua's eyes, and when that happened, he stopped shaking and his eyes seemed to brighten. Joshua gave him the sandwich his mother had given to him when he left without eating breakfast.

"Eat this, Jimmy, and come with me to school. I will stay with you. Don't be afraid. No one will know what happened, so don't be self-conscious. If we go to school right now, we should be on time, but we'll have to walk fast."

"Thank you, Joshua. You are my best friend. You are so different from everyone else, so good, so different, you make me feel at peace, and you make me feel strong."

"I will talk to my Father in heaven about your mother and father. You should talk to my Father in heaven, too, Jimmy. He is also your Father in heaven. He will listen to you. He always listens, especially to prayers that come from a broken heart."

The two boys walked to school together. As they entered, Jimmy asked Joshua, "Do you think the kids will suspect something?"

"Not if you act normal as if nothing happened. They have no reason to think anything."

"Do I look okay?"

"You look fine. Stop worrying about it. Just go into your class as if everything is normal, and I will see you at lunch break."

The two parted.

Joshua got to his class just in time.

"Good morning, Joshua. How's my little friend?" Miss Axeman said with a smile.

"Good morning, Miss Axeman," Joshua responded with a twinkle in his eye.

As Joshua sat down at his desk, he closed his eyes and talked to his Father in heaven, asking him to protect his friend Jimmy and make him strong, and also to give his parents the grace to love each other. His prayers were always brief, but he knew they went right to his Father's heart.

His short prayer ended when he heard the teacher call his name.

"Joshua, would you come up to the blackboard and write out the names of the fifty states. Since they are not in one place in your textbook, I want everyone to have a complete list. I would like all the others to copy down each state as you write it on the board, so the others will have a list they can use and commit to memory. A friend told me that you know them, and I am sure it will be fun for you to write them out for the class."

Joshua was embarrassed, but glad that he had learned

them all on his own. He did not particularly like being singled out in front of the class, which he thought was the teacher's way of giving him practice at writing cursive. After he began writing the names of the states, one by one, he felt proud of himself and began to enjoy it.

To everyone's surprise, he wrote them all down without hesitation. To his embarrassment the whole class clapped when he finished and walked back to his seat.

"Thank you, Joshua. That was well done, and I notice your cursive is vastly improved."

"Thank you," he responded.

His mind was still on his friend, hoping he was coping with his class. He couldn't wait till noon so he could meet with him.

As soon as lunchtime came, he went directly to Jimmy's class to wait for him. But he did not come out. He asked his teacher if Jimmy was inside.

"No, Joshua, I haven't seen him all morning."

Joshua was beside himself. Where had Jimmy gone? What had happened to him? Was he hurt? Joshua was shattered. He walked directly to Jimmy's house to see if he had gone home. His mother had not seen him since he left for school earlier. She was beside herself, wondering what had happened to him.

Joshua left and went all over the village trying to find his friend, hoping that nothing tragic had happened to him.

"Father, help me find Jimmy. He needs me, Father. I can't let anything happen to him. Please help me find him, Father."

After looking every possible place he could think of, he decided to walk down near the railroad tracks, and, walking quietly through thick weeds, he saw his friend with two other boys, both much older than Jimmy. One of them

Joshua recognized as a boy whose family had recently moved to the village. From the start Joshua had had an uneasy feeling about the boy. He knew immediately that he was the one who was giving drugs to Jimmy. Joshua's anger began to rise, but he kept calm and slowly walked over to the group, and called to Jimmy.

"Who's that guy?" the new boy in town asked Jimmy.

"He's my friend." Jimmy was filled with shame when he saw Joshua and did not know what to do.

As Joshua approached, the boy whom Joshua did not know asked him, "What are you lookin' for?"

"I'm looking for my friend."

"You'd better move on, if you know what's good for you. He's stayin' here with us."

"He's coming with me," Joshua said firmly.

"You're lookin' for trouble, wise guy. Well, you're gonna get it," the stranger said.

Undeterred, Joshua looked at Jimmy. "Come on, Jimmy, let's go back home."

"He ain't leavin'."

The new boy in town went over to Joshua and tried to hit him, but missed when Joshua made a quick move. Then Joshua grabbed the boy by the back of the neck and did something that made him fall to the ground. He lay there, motionless.

"Jimmy, let's go," Joshua said. "I don't like fighting, so let's get out of here."

The other boy, seeing what had happened to his companion, made no move toward Joshua. Jimmy left the two others and walked down the tracks with Joshua. As they walked away, the boy Joshua had tangled with was beginning to come to and was trying to get up.

"Have those two given drugs to other kids in the village, Jimmy?"

Jimmy was afraid to say anything, but finally he broke down and confessed that there were at least five others to whom they gave drugs. "They give them out free at first, and now they want us to pay for them. I'm so scared, Joshua. I don't have any money. I'd have to steal it if I was going to pay them, and I don't want to do anything bad like that."

"You have to be honest with me, Jimmy, and promise to keep away from those boys. They will destroy your whole life. I will help you, but you have to stay with me and not play games with me."

"I will, Joshua. I'm so afraid."

When they went inside Jimmy's house, Jimmy's mother was on the phone, calling everyone she knew and asking if they had seen her son. As soon as the boys entered the kitchen, she turned on Jimmy and demanded to know where he had been and what had happened.

Jimmy was shaking like a leaf. Joshua spoke up, telling his mother, "Jimmy unintentionally got into trouble by trusting some boys who are new in the area. He's all upset and needs you to help him. It's not going to help if you holler at him. He's scared enough."

"What happened, Son?"

"Mother, these boys gave me drugs. I didn't know what they were, and when I took them they made me feel good and made me forget about you and dad fighting. But now I realize that it was evil to be involved with those fellows, and I want to do what's right. I know Joshua will help me, too. He's my best friend, and kept looking for me until he found me."

"Joshua, I am grateful to you for bringing my son home to me. You are a wonderful example to the other children in town. I am proud that my son is your friend."

"Mrs. Cronin, Jimmy is a rare good boy. That's why I like him so much. He is very sensitive and can be easily hurt. I know it tears him apart inside when there is no peace at home. He can't sleep nights and doesn't even want to eat. I know you love your son and will do what you have to to protect him from the terrible things that can happen."

She was ashamed that a boy so young should have to make her realize that she could be a better mother, and it brought tears to her eyes. She walked over and hugged Jimmy, to show Joshua that she really did love him and care for him.

Mrs. Cronin made lunch for the two boys. When they finished, they walked back to school for afternoon classes and acted as if nothing had happened. But the afternoon was not an easy experience for either of them. Jimmy was already experiencing the restlessness that comes with addiction. Joshua was anxious for his friend, even though he knew that his Father in heaven was going to help Jimmy conquer the problem. The source of the evil that was threatening to destroy the whole village was the newcomers. They created demand for the drugs by giving free samples until the kids became addicted; then the kids would steal and do almost anything to get money to satisfy their destructive craving. Joshua, young as he was, was still shrewd and knew that he had to ask his Father in heaven to do something to eliminate the source of the problem. He prayed all during class that his Father would help him. By the end of the afternoon he had a plan.

When he met Jimmy after classes, he drew enough information from him to figure out where his new friends were keeping their supply of drugs. When Jimmy went home, Joshua went looking for the drugs and, knowing the young dealers would be meeting with students after class, he found the cache and then went to the police station to talk to a detective, whose son was one of Joshua's friends.

Joshua asked the detective if he could talk to him privately.

"Of course, Joshua. What's on that active little mind of yours?"

"I have a very serious problem, Sergeant Spaulding. You have to help me, and *all* the kids in town."

"How's that, Joshua?"

"There are some newcomers in town passing out drugs to the kids, and some kids are already getting hooked on them. I found where the batch of drugs is being kept, and if you can go to the place and take them, then the kids who are selling them will get into trouble with the people who are supplying them. If you and some of the other policemen keep a watch on who comes in to meet with the new kids who are pushing them, then you can arrest them and stop the drugs from coming into the village."

"Can you show me where the drugs are now?"

"Yes, but you won't arrest any of the kids, will you, Sergeant Spaulding?"

"No, Joshua. We will just arrest the adults who are supplying them, but we'll put the boys under constant surveillance for their own good, and for their protection as well."

Joshua showed the detective where the boxes of drugs were hidden, in a shed behind one of the boys' house. Sergeant Spaulding was delighted at the find and immediately got back to the police chief, and together they planned a stakeout. After obtaining the proper warrants and other necessary papers, they picked up the drugs and laid the trap.

They knew that the criminals would be after their young local pushers, and sure enough, later that evening just after suppertime, when the two boys left their home, the police were sure they were going to a rendezvous to meet the criminals. It turned out to be a wooded lot on a back road just outside the village. The police positioned themselves at a safe distance in the heavy brush, which provided enough cover for themselves and their surveillance equipment.

At eight o'clock sharp, an ordinary-looking car drove up within a hundred feet of where the boys were waiting. Sergeant Spaulding turned on an electronic eavesdropping device that could pick up the conversation between the boys and the suspects who had just gotten out of the car and were approaching the boys.

"What's this story you told us that you don't have the packages?"

"They just disappeared. We had them hidden, and when we went to get them, they weren't there."

"Don't give me that."

"Honest, mister, we don't have them. We looked all over for them. They just disappeared. We kept them behind the shed in my back yard, and now they're gone."

One of the men started beating one of the boys in an attempt to force the other one to talk, but even when he saw his friend all bloody, he still insisted they did not have the packages.

"But we have the money for the rest of the drugs we sold, and here are the packages we have left."

The boys handed the money and the drugs over to the men, and at that point Sergeant Spaulding left the equipment running to record what was happening. He and three other policemen rushed over with guns drawn and surrounded the shocked suspects. Knowing there was no way to escape, the men surrendered quietly. The police already had enough evidence to arrest them on drug charges as well as for assaulting the boy.

Sergeant Spaulding opened a brown paper bag and asked the boys if the packages in the bag were what they were looking for. They immediately, without even thinking, shouted out to the two men, "Here's the packages that were lost, mister, the ones you wanted."

The men ignored the boys, but they knew the police had hard evidence, as their fingerprints were all over the packages. Two of the officers made the men lie facedown on the ground while Sergeant Spaulding called for help. The fourth officer stayed with the two boys and handcuffed them as well. One of the boys peed in his pants. The other boy laughed nervously when he saw what was happening to his companion.

Within five minutes three police cars arrived and took the four policemen, the two drug dealers, and the boys to the Shadybrook police station. The men were booked, photographed, and fingerprinted, then driven off in the sheriff's car to the county jail. The two boys were kept in the village cell until the police notified their parents, who rushed to the jail in total panic, not believing what was happening to their children. The policemen told the parents that they would have to contact the judge, who would make any further decisions about the boys. They also told the parents they would not have to worry about the men who were arrested. They would be out of circulation permanently, and the parents could rest assured these pushers would not be bothering the kids in town any longer.

When the judge finally arrived about forty-five minutes later, he decided the boys could go home with their parents, and he would let the parents know in a week or so what his determination would be concerning the fate of their sons. Although he intended to give them another chance, knowing the police would be keeping a sharp eye on them both from now on, he did not tell this to the parents. He wanted them and the boys to do some heavy soul-searching during that time.

It was late when the session ended. No one else in the village even knew what had happened, though there were rumors circulating that a number of police cars were involved in picking up strangers who had driven into town. People did suspect there might have been drugs involved. The police did, as a matter of fact, find more drugs while searching the strangers' car.

After meeting earlier after school with Sergeant Spaulding, Joshua went home. He was a little late, which again made his mother worry.

"Son, where were you? Didn't you know your father and I would be worrying about you since we saw you so upset when you left this morning?"

"I am sorry, Mother. I really had some important things to do that could not wait. As soon as I finished, I came right home," Joshua told her as he walked over to her and hugged her hard, kissing her on both cheeks. "I love you, Mother. I'm sorry I caused you worry."

"I know you are, Joshua. But please be careful. I cannot let anything happen to you. Is everything all right? You were so troubled this morning."

"Yes, everything worked out well. I know my Father in heaven answered my prayers. He always answers my prayers. So I feel all at peace now, and my friend Jimmy is safe."

Joshua knew that his mother was really interested in knowing what it was all about, but she thought it best not to ask. Knowing she was concerned, Joshua promised to tell her all about it first chance he got, but his big interest now was getting something to eat.

"Mother, I am famished. I have to have something to eat."

"We have all kinds of food in the refrigerator. Take what you like but don't spoil your appetite. We'll be having supper in a little while."

After making a sandwich with cold cuts his father liked, he went out to the back yard and picked an apple from an old tree at the end of the property. His father was working on the boat, but said nothing. Joshua knew he was concerned about his son not coming home immediately after school, especially since he was supposed to help him with the boat.

"Father, I'm sorry I came home late. There was a terrible problem with my good friend Jimmy. He was in a lot of trouble and I had to help him. I could not leave him by himself. But everything turned out well, and Jimmy is safe. I came home as fast as I could."

"I was worried, Son. But I'm glad everything turned out well. Now, let's get working here. Hold this board in place while I secure it."

The strips of wood that had been soaking were bent to perfect shape, and Joseph screwed them into place one by one, securing them tightly with epoxy so there would be no leaks. With the new materials, it was easy to put a boat together in a few days and have it be perfectly waterproof.

All that was left was the painting, and the naming, of the vessel, which they would accomplish next day after school.

"That's a beautiful boat, Father. Are we going to make oars?"

"Go over to my shed and see what's in there."

"Father, there are oars, and a sail, too. And what's this thing?"

Joshua held up a contraption he did not recognize.

"That's the rudder, in case we want to use the sail. I made it so we can attach it easily if we need it for sailing. There's also a little trolling motor in there with a propeller on it, which we can also use when we go fishing. It won't scare away the fish like rowing does."

"I can't wait to take it down to the lake and go for a ride."

"Maybe the day after tomorrow."

It was suppertime, and they went inside to clean up.

At supper Joshua told his parents the whole story of what had happened during the day. They were even more concerned when they found out there was such dangerous activity among the children in their quiet little village. It seemed that no place was safe from the horrible things spreading across the country.

JOSHUA WOKE UP THE NEXT MORNING IN A HAPPY
mood. His mother could tell when she heard him
whistling to the birds on his windowsill.

"I guess he slept a dreamless sleep last night," Joseph said
to his wife as a broad grin crossed his face.

"That child! He sure is a mystery, Joseph. I'm glad he's
happy today. I hope he has a peaceful day. I know he's happy
most of the time, but some days it is almost as if he carries
the weight of the world on his little shoulders. Thank God
he bounces back fast. Listen to him whistling away as if he
doesn't have a care in the world. It's as if nothing happened
yesterday."

"He certainly doesn't lack for excitement," Joseph added.

"Don't forget to come down for breakfast, Joshua. We're
all ready," his mother called up to him.

"Be right down, Mother."

And in no time he was rushing down the stairs, taking
two at a time.

"Joshua, please don't do that. One of these days you're going to trip and really get hurt."

No sooner had the words left Miriam's mouth than Joshua tripped on the last two steps and fell flat on his face, scraping his chin on the rug.

Miriam turned and with a panicked look asked if he was hurt.

"Mother, I'm not hurt. It was only two steps. I'm okay."

"Son, I don't want you to ever do that again. It is so dangerous. You could break your neck if you ever miss the top steps."

Joseph just watched and said nothing. His face showed his concern, which Joshua did not miss.

The exciting thing in school that day was the class's introduction to the new computers the district had sent to the school for the fourth graders. Previously only those in the fifth grade and up had had computers. Joshua had wondered about those things and could not wait to learn all about them.

Right from the start he threw himself into the computer work. In class he was all eyes and ears, absorbing instantly everything the instructor said and following on his computer each direction the teacher gave, making sure he got it right. What fascinated him most was the computer's ability to communicate with what the teacher called the Internet, where the user could not only tap into a whole new world of information and learn about things in distant lands, and about people in othe parts of the world, but could also contact other people on computers thousands of miles away, and immediately. That really fascinated him.

His quick mind saw all kinds of possibilities, and after the class's first lesson Joshua was totally captivated. He couldn't wait for the next computer class so he could learn more, and he asked the instructor if there was a book he could borrow so he could study at home. The instructor was impressed with the young lad's enthusiasm and readily lent him a manual, which he could browse as deeply as his mind could absorb.

Even though Joshua loved to learn, the computer totally fired his imagination. When he went home after school, he was excited to help his father with the boat, but spent most of the time while they were working telling his father about computers. Of course, Joseph knew nothing about what his son was telling him.

"These computers, Joshua, what are they, boxes like radios, or television sets?"

"Something like that, Abba, but different. You can write letters to people, and you can talk through them like a telephone, and you can do all kinds of things with them."

"I can see you are excited about them, but I have to admit, Son, I really can't even imagine what you are trying to tell me. Maybe someday I may be able to see one, then I might be able to understand what you're talking about."

"I can't bring one home, but if you come to school someday, maybe I can show you."

"That would be nice. Now, let's finish up our work on the boat so we can show your mother. What do you think we should name it?"

"How about *Joseph's Ark*?"

"No, that's to corny, as the kids would say."

"How about *Peter the Fisherman*?"

"That's clever, but let's try another one."

"How about *Star of the Sea*, in honor of Mother, who's always bright and cheerful even in dark, troubled times?"

"That's good, but let's shorten it to *Bright Star* in honor of your mother. That's what she is, always a bright star to both of us."

"That's a good idea, Abba. *Bright Star*. I like that. Mother will like it, too. I can't wait to ride in it now that it's finished."

"Maybe tomorrow. Let's put the sail on it and surprise your mother after supper, though I think she may have been peeking out the window at our progress, even though we tried to keep out of sight."

It was almost time for supper. Joshua and his father washed up, and after coming back downstairs, Joshua started telling his mother all about computers. Of course, she knew nothing about what he was telling her, but she listened politely.

"I have no idea what a computer is, Son, but I can tell that you like it, whatever it is. I hope it doesn't distract you from your other schoolwork."

"No; in fact, it can help me with my other schoolwork. I can study on the computer and learn all kinds of things."

When Joseph came into the kitchen, Miriam asked if he knew what a computer was.

"Only what our little student told me. It's sort of like a box, or a television, or a telephone. But I have to admit, I can't even imagine what it could look like."

Joshua laughed. "It's everything you said, Father, except it also has a keyboard like a typewriter."

"Joshua, now you have me totally baffled. I'm afraid I am going to have to stick to my carpentry. That's about all I know, except for the history of our people and all the blessings bestowed upon us."

With that, Joseph kissed Miriam tenderly on the cheek. Joshua smiled.

"We have a surprise for you, Mother, after supper," Joshua said.

"I can't wait. So, let's sit down and eat so you can show me before it gets dark outside."

Even Joseph was excited about the surprise they had in store for Miriam, and couldn't wait until they finished supper.

"Now, Mother," Joshua said. "You close your eyes, and no peeking. Hold my hand and I will lead you out into the back yard."

Joseph smiled at seeing his son, such a simple child and so full of excitement.

Holding his mother's hand, he led her over to the boat and then said, "Okay, Mother, you can open your eyes now."

"Joseph, Joshua, it is beautiful. I love that sail. And the seats look so comfortable. Can I sit in it?

"Well, no. It's not quite ready yet," Joshua replied. "But I am so glad you like it. See the name on it. We named it after you. You are our bright star, always so bright and cheerful even when times are dark."

Tears welled up in Miriam's eyes as she walked over and hugged them both, saying to them tenderly, "Thank you. I love you two beautiful men in my life."

They christened the new ship by breaking open a bottle of sparkling apple cider, which Miriam served with home-made chocolate cookies baked with dried cherries.

When Joshua went to bed, he had so many new things to be thankful for. He stood at his bedroom window, looking out at the heavens where a full moon was shining brightly. Holding his hands up to his Father in heaven, he told him about all the things that had happened over the past few days and about how exciting and frightening and joyful they all were. He thanked him for his wonderful mother who was so full of love and understanding, especially when he did things that he knew must frighten her, and for his father who was such a dear friend and excellent craftsman, and gentle father.

He thanked him for having a father who could be his friend and let him work with him when he made things, especially things they could enjoy together, like the wonderful boat, which he could not wait to ride in the next day. Finally, he prayed for all his friends and for all the troubled kids, that his Father in heaven would bless them and protect them and keep them safe.

When he finished his long prayer, he was excited about so many things, it took him a while to relax enough to go to sleep, but when he did, it was the sleep of the blessed.

He was the first one up the next morning, and after talking to his bird friends at the feeder, he went downstairs and surprised everyone by having breakfast ready for them when they came down.

"Joshua, what a nice surprise!" his mother said with mild shock in her voice.

"And the eggs and the bacon are prepared to perfection," Joseph added.

"That's to say 'thank you' for all the nice things you do for me every day," Joshua added as he poured cherry juice into the glasses.

"Yahweh, our Father in heaven," Joseph began the prayer, "we thank you from the bottom of our hearts for all the blessings you pour so lavishly into our lives. May we show our gratitude by sharing with others who are in need, and who need to know that you care for them. And bless this food that our son Joshua prepared so nicely for us all this morning. Bless his day, and may his love of learning increase each day, as his love for you grows in his heart."

To which they all added their amen.

Joshua sang softly to himself as he walked to school.

"You seem like a happy spirit," Marguerite said as she quietly walked up behind him.

"Oh, hi, Marguerite. I haven't seen you in so long. Where have you been?"

"I've been around, but now that you are in a different class, we rarely see each other. But I look for you and think of you a lot. You've been really busy lately, haven't you?"

Joshua did not know what to say or how to answer. He knew Marguerite had her way of finding out practically everything that he did. He hoped she didn't know about the latest episode with Jimmy. He didn't want that spread around the village.

"I've been keeping busy. My father and I just finished making a boat. Maybe someday you can come for a ride with us down on the lake."

"You made a boat, a real boat?"

"Yes, my father can make anything. He is an excellent craftsman. And I helped him, too, so we really made it together."

"How big is it?"

"It's about twenty feet long, and it has a sail, and also a little trolling motor, my father calls it, so it doesn't scare the fish when we go fishing."

"I would love to have a ride in it someday."

"Okay, I'll talk to my mother and dad about it, and I am sure they would be happy for you to come with us. They like you very much, you know."

"I know, and I like them, too. Well, have a good time in school today, Joshua, and I hope I see you again real soon. You know you're my best friend."

"I know, and I'm yours, too, Marguerite. Enjoy your day."

As Joshua walked up the path to the school entrance, Jimmy came running up to him.

"Hi, Joshua. Thank you for all you did, especially for having touched my parents' hearts."

"What did I do, Jimmy?"

"I don't know, but ever since you came to the house, my mother, and my father, too, have been so different. It's almost as if they like each other the way they used to a long time ago. And it makes me feel a lot happier. Thank you for whatever you did, Joshua. I heard your class got new computers. Do you like them?"

"They're great. I have so much fun with the computer. I'm learning all I can about them so I can use them better. They're very complicated."

"I wish I could learn how to use a computer. My father has a computer, but he uses it for work."

"Maybe if you ask him, he'll teach you how to use it."

"I'll ask him. Have a good day, Joshua. I'll see you later."

"You have a good day, too, Jimmy. And don't forget to talk to your Father in heaven. He loves you," Joshua added with a broad smile.

"I think I know what you mean. Someone's protecting me."

Walking down the corridor to his classroom, Joshua met Miss Axeman.

"How's my young friend," she greeted him, which always caused Joshua to blush.

"Fine, Miss Axeman."

"I hear you are all excited about your new computers. The computer teacher is already expecting great things of you."

"Yes, I think they're fascinating. I can't wait to learn more about them. I can tell there's so much we can do with computers, but they're not very good at writing cursive," Joshua said with a grin.

The teacher did not miss his humor.

"That's a good one, Joshua. I have to admit, you really are good at cursive. I smile when I think of the first day. I guess I was a little hard on you."

"That was nothing. I really wanted to learn cursive fast. It's much nicer than printing."

The two walked into the classroom together, and one of the girls remarked, "Oh, here comes the teacher's pet."

Everyone knew Miss Axeman liked Joshua, and even though he was happy she did, because he liked her, it still embarrassed him.

School was becoming more and more fun with each passing day. His friends were not as interested in their schoolwork. They were good summertime playmates and were good in sports. Fourth-graders weren't into basketball and football yet, so Joshua's friends hung around the village or took the bus and went to the mall, which was not very far. There they could hang out or go to the movies, or just keep busy. They were all good kids, and not the type who would look for trouble. When they got together with Joshua they were always friendly and enjoyed talking about the great times they had during the summer and how they couldn't wait till summer came back so they could play together.

Now that Joshua was into computers, he had an interest that would keep him busy all during the cold winter months when there wasn't much that could be done outside.

After his first class with Miss Axeman, he couldn't wait for his computer class. They were going to learn about dial-up and broadband and how they could be used to do research on the Internet. Joshua asked question after question, making sure he understood everything the instructor said. Mr.

Conrad was the instructor, and he enjoyed the vast curiosity of this young student who could never learn enough.

"What do we have in class, Mr. Conrad, dial-up or broadband?" he asked.

"We have broadband. It is much faster than dial-up. When you are searching, you will find broadband to be much more to your liking. You don't have to wait to find what you're looking for. Most of the time it is almost instantaneous."

"How do you use the computer as a telephone?"

"If the computer has a microphone and speakers, as ours do, you have all you need. You use the special software already in the computer and just dial the phone number. When someone answers, you talk to the person. It's simple, just like a telephone."

"I think we are going to get a telephone in our house. We don't have one yet, but I think it might be good to have one, so I can call my friends, and also so people can call my father to do work for them. I think my mother would also like to talk to her friends, too."

"You don't have a phone in your house, Joshua? I thought everybody had telephones," Charlie, one of Joshua's friends, blurted out.

"We never needed one before, but I think we're going to need one soon."

Mr. Conrad smiled at Joshua's simplicity, which was so rare and refreshing.

The class went by fast, too fast, and before long, school was out, and Joshua went home immediately, so he and his father and mother could make their maiden voyage on the lake.

Getting the boat down to the lake was going to be a problem, Joshua thought, but by the time he got home, his father already had that problem solved. One of the men at the lumberyard, a friend of Joseph's named Mickey, had told Joseph that he had old bicycles he wanted to get rid of, and if he knew of anyone who could use them, they were welcome to them. In fact, he kept them in the back of his truck for immediate disposal, and when Joseph told him he could use them, Mickey was nice enough to drop them off at Joseph's house at lunchtime. When Joseph told him that he really needed the wheels and showed him the boat he had made, Mickey could not believe his eyes.

"Yes, my son Joshua and I built that boat ourselves, and we are going for a boat ride down at the lake this afternoon. My only problem was, I did not know how we were going to get the boat down there. You've solved that for us. Now I can make a little flatbed and pull the boat down the street. Mickey, I know you like to fish, so if you would like to use the boat sometime to go fishing, you are welcome to it."

"Thanks, Joseph. I've been too busy lately, but first chance I get, I'll take you up on that. Well, I know you have the afternoon off, but I have to get back to work, so I'll see you tomorrow. Bon voyage!"

"Thank you, and thank you so much for the bicycles."

"I'm glad you could use them. You took them off my hands."

By the time Joshua returned from school, the flatbed was all finished and the boat was firmly secured on it. All that was needed now was to secure Miriam to her commitment to join them in the boat ride.

It wasn't long before Joshua came running breathlessly down the street. This was their big day. Joseph had just finished moving the flatbed out into the front yard, and all was ready. Now to make sure that Miriam was ready, too.

"Father, where's Mother? She didn't change her mind, did she?"

"I hope not. I think she's coming. Why don't you go in and tell her we're all ready. I know you can persuade her. You're good at that."

Running into the house, he almost ran his mother down. She had just come down the stairs and was walking toward the door when Joshua came bursting into the room.

"Oh, Mother, you're all ready. Father and I were wondering if you were all ready to come with us on our maiden voyage."

"Joshua, I don't know whether I can swim."

"Mother, we're not going swimming. We're going for a boat ride."

"I know, but what if the boat tips over and we fall in the water."

"Mother, the boat's not going to tip over, and if it does I will save you. Nothing can happen to you when you're with me. Don't you know that?"

"Joshua, I know you're brave, and I trust you, but we're going to have to be very careful."

"I promise, Mother, and besides, Father is always super-careful when it concerns you."

The three of them walked down the road, with Joseph and Joshua pulling the flatbed with the boat riding proudly on top, the sail full mast. It was quite a sight. Joshua was so proud. It was too bad his friends could not be there with him to see the parade. They would certainly be impressed with this beautiful piece of workmanship floating proudly down the old back road.

When they reached the pond, Joseph, not wanting Miriam to get wet, made a gallant gesture to carry her to the boat, but she would not even hear of it. Taking off her sandals, she walked into the water and, with a little help from her husband, took the seat in the front of the boat.

"Joshua, you're next. Take one of the seats up toward the front. I'll sit in the back here and work the tiller. Then after a while you can take the tiller. We're lucky today. There is just enough of a breeze to push us gently across the lake."

"Abba, this boat is beautiful. How did you ever learn how to make boats?"

"Joshua, a carpenter in the old days didn't just cut wood. He had to be able to do all kinds of things, even work with metal, to make plows and door hinges, and wheels. Making this boat was fun. Knowing how to do something is the secret."

"Father, I want to be like you when I get big."

"Thank you, Son, but I think your Father in heaven has special plans for you. Your mother and I are just your guardians, not your role models. You are very special to your Father in heaven."

"I don't understand, Abba."

"I know, Son. One day you will."

Miriam looked anxious. Joseph noticed and smiled. "Dear," he said gently, "you look nice and comfortable, and relaxed."

"Relaxed? I'm not very relaxed. I've never ridden in a boat before, and I've always wondered why they don't tip over."

"The keel underneath the boat keeps it steady and prevents it from tilting from side to side. That's why the ride is so smooth."

"I do feel a little more relaxed than I did when I first got in. And, it does ride easily. I think it could be fun."

Joshua looked at his mother with an impish grin. He was always used to seeing his mother so properly composed. To see her anxious and a little nervous was almost humorous. She noticed his grin and snapped jokingly, "Joshua, stop that impish grin. I know what you're thinking."

"I can't help it, Mother. You look comical when you're anxious like that."

At that they all laughed and it broke the ice. For the rest of the voyage they were all relaxed and had great fun. The breeze was so gentle the boat hardly tilted at all, and for almost an hour they just sailed ever so peacefully around the lake.

"Now, Joseph, I can see why Peter and John and the others had so much fun as fishermen so long ago."

"That was quite a bit different, Miriam. The Sea of Galilee is a lot different from this quiet lake. The waters in Galilee could be stirred up violently by the powerful winds rushing down from Lake Huleh in the north, causing violent storms on the sea. That could be real trouble."

"Well, I'm glad I never took a ride in Peter's boat then. I would have been really scared."

"Abba, can I steer the boat?"

"Okay, but be careful coming back here. Don't stand up, just stay squatted and work your way to where I am, and I will move up and take your place."

His father continued, "Now, Joshua, when you want to steer to the right, you move the tiller to the left, and when you want to go to the left, you move the tiller to the right."

"This is fun, Abba. This is real fun."

Miriam just smiled. She was happy to see her two men being such good friends and all of them having such a happy time together.

"Mother, would you like to steer the boat?"

"No, Son, it is more fun just watching you two."

They sailed for almost an hour, then worked their way

back to the pond and to the flatbed. They were like three little kids walking back to the house, pulling the boat behind them. Joshua felt so proud, and even though he was more reserved in showing it, so was Joseph.

"Supper will be ready in about half and hour, so when you two are finished putting the boat back in the yard and get cleaned up, it will all be ready. Supper tonight is my "Thank you" to both of you for treating me to such a wonderful afternoon."

"We were hoping you'd enjoy it," Joseph told her.

"I did, and I would even like doing it again sometime, if you wouldn't mind taking me."

"That would be great, Mother. Would you mind if Father and I go fishing first, because I don't think you would like fishing."

"You are very thoughtful, Joshua," Miriam said with a grin, knowing that he was looking forward to fishing with his father. "You go fishing first, and next time I'll go with you."

F ALL WEATHER WAS BEGINNING TO BRING A CHILL
to the air, which shortened the time for sailing. Joshua
did get a few chances to bring his friends sailing. He also
went fishing with his father, and it was always Joseph who
caught the fish. Joshua never seemed to have any luck. He
was genuinely disappointed. He did, however, manage to
drag up various articles from the bottom of the lake, which
made the both of them break into laughter. Even though he
was disappointed, Joshua could still see the humor in it, and
he laughed along with his father. Joseph's fish were big
enough to provide a hearty supper for the three of them,
anyway. On two occasions they docked the boat at the old
man's place and gave him one of the fish they had caught.
On the first occasion, he was so surprised at the nice gesture
that he cried and thanked them. He was not used to people
doing nice things like that for him.

"That son of yours, Joseph, is quite a lad. He stops over
here every now and then and cuts my lawn. The other day

he raked the leaves. He is the only one who has ever done that for me. He is so thoughtful, and I sure do appreciate it. I am too weak to do that anymore. There isn't much I can do, now that I am old. It is not easy growing old, especially when you live alone."

"But, Mr. Jeremy, you're not alone. Your Father in heaven is with you all the time. He takes care of you when there is no one else to care for you. He's the one who told me that I should visit you and help you. So, you see, you are not alone. And if you need us, just call my name and I will hear you. I can always tell when someone needs me."

"You see, Joseph, why I love that boy. He is so special. He is so unlike the other children in the village. He is kind to everyone, even to those whom I can tell are not nice to him. When I take my occasional walks to the village, I keep my eyes open, and my ears, too. I see a lot. I see the way some kids treat Joshua. He is most unusual. He must have a strong sense of who he is, because nothing that they say seems to upset him. He just shrugs it off and still treats them in a friendly way. Amazing boy!"

"I know that, Jeremy, and he is a big help to me, too, but, Jeremy, let me tell you, he can be a handful sometimes. He likes to pull practical tricks around the house. I'll have to tell you about them sometime."

Jeremy Lockhart looked forward to the brief visits from his new friends. They brightened up his day, and even though Joshua was only a young boy, he said things to the old man that made a lot of sense and brought him considerable comfort and peace, and took away much of the fear and anxiety that is a great part of old age, especially when one realizes that the last days cannot be very far away.

But old Jeremy Lockhart was not the only one whom Joshua helped. There were other old folks in the village who were unable to do even ordinary chores. Joshua noticed them, too, as he walked around the village.

One day, on his way to visit his friend Jimmy, he saw an old lady sweeping her sidewalk. She suddenly put her hand up to her chest and dropped the broom. Joshua could see she looked very weak. He ran over to her and told her to hold on to him so she wouldn't fall. Shocked at this young boy's astute awareness of her condition, she held on to him until she got her balance and then walked with him back into the house.

"Thank you, young man. I think you saved my life. I knew I was going to fall, and if I fell I probably would have hit my head and died."

The woman wanted to give him some money, but Joshua looked so offended, she ended up apologizing and invited him to have a cup of tea with her instead, which he readily accepted.

"I do appreciate your offering to give me something, Mrs. Smith, but I never had much interest in money. I find more joy in helping you. I know it is not easy for older people, so if you ever need me, just call my name and I will hear you and come and help you."

"That is so thoughtful of you, young man. You mean I should call you on the telephone?"

"No, we do not have a telephone. Just call my name. You don't have to say it out loud. I will hear you and come to you."

"How remarkable! How will you know I am thinking of you or calling you?"

"I don't know, but I just have that ability to know when someone needs me. I guess it must be a gift my Father in heaven gave me so I could help people who need me."

Then Joshua remembered his mother telling him not to tell others about the gifts his Father in heaven had given him, but it was too late. He had already let it slip out.

"What is your name?" she asked him.

"Joshua."

"Thank you so much, Joshua. What a beautiful name! It means Jesus, in English. I think he must have been like you when he was on earth a long time ago."

Joshua smiled and told the lady he had things to do, so he excused himself, said good-bye, and left.

Mrs. Smith sat there looking into the tea leaves at the bottom of her cup, wondering how this strange boy could know her name when she had never met him before.

It did not take long before Joshua's reputation spread among the very old folks who had little else to do but spend hours on the phone with each other, sharing the little dramas that gave meaning to their lonely, fragile lives. As there were not very many really old folks in town, it was easy for Joshua to visit them all and still have time for his friends, who knew nothing about this very private part of his life.

Joshua had become a favorite topic among the old folks. They liked him. He was their sunshine, and he had a warm feeling about each one of them. They were vulnerable and often found life frightening as they became more and more frail. It pained him to see them trying to do chores around their houses, knowing that merely falling down could be life-threatening to them. So, he enjoyed visiting them, making sure they had enough to eat, and seeing that they were in good health.

One day he visited a really elderly lady. Marianna Azzam was ninety-two and in relatively good health. She shared with Joshua that she would be taking a trip soon to go to her great-grandson's graduation from college. She had been dreaming about that for years. Now it was not far off. She hoped her health would hold up until the graduation.

Joshua promised to pray for her that her dream would come true.

"Thank you, young man. Thank you. I know God will hear your prayers. You are so innocent, and so good. I pray for you every day, that God will protect you and keep you from harm, and that your life will be blessed."

As the time for graduation approached, Joshua went to visit the woman. She was not feeling well and had not been able to eat for the last few days. The doctor, an old friend, came to visit her and told her she would have to go into the hospital for tests. She was reluctant for fear the doctors might find something that would prevent her from going to her great-grandson's graduation.

That evening an ambulance drove her to the hospital. The next day, after a battery of tests, it was determined that she had cancer, a cancer that was so far advanced, there was little the doctors could do for her. The poor soul was devastated.

Somehow Joshua knew that something had happened to her and that she needed him. Knowing that he should go visit her, he told his parents, and they suggested that he pray for the woman. But he insisted that it was important that he visit her, that she needed him to visit her, and that Marguerite's mother and father would be glad to take him as they were going to visit her the next day. His parents felt comfortable with that, so they consented to let him go.

When he entered her hospital room, she brightened up immediately.

"Joshua, Joshua, you *did* know that I needed you! Oh, I am so happy that you have come. I have such bad news. The doctor told me that I have cancer very bad, and there is little they can do for me. I feel terrible that I can't be at my young William's graduation. It looks like I am going to die."

Knowing how the old lady felt about Joshua, Marguerite's mother and father let Joshua have a few minutes alone with the woman so she could pour her heart out to him, though they could hear every word being said.

"Marianna, do not be afraid. I know how much faith you have in my Father in heaven. He is your Father, too, you know. I prayed to him and asked him to heal you, and my Father always answers my prayers. So don't be afraid. You will still be able to go to William's graduation."

"I hope so, child. I hope so."

At that point the other visitors came into the room. Marianna was thrilled to see them. Joshua kissed the old lady on the forehead and stepped back from the bed so the others could come closer to greet the woman.

When they left the hospital, Joshua sat in the backseat for the ride home, which would take less than an hour.

"Thank you for bringing me with you to see Mrs. Azzam," Joshua said to Mr. and Mrs. McCabe. "I would not have been able to come if you were not so kind. She is a nice lady, and our visit meant a lot to her."

"Joshua, we were glad to take you. We have all become very fond of you over the past few months. You are an unusual boy, and just your presence makes a big difference in our community. You are a good example for the other children because you have a strong character and are not a sissy or afraid of anybody, and you obviously have your own mind. A lot of the other children look up to you. Just listening to the kids talk, we can tell that they respect you. They know that you care for each of them, and that's unusual in a boy so young."

When Joshua did not reply, Mrs. McCabe turned around to look back at him. He was sound asleep, curled up in the corner of the seat, snoring quietly.

Bill and Vivian talked in a low voice the rest of the way home so they wouldn't disturb their sleeping passenger, but a passing ambulance with siren screaming woke him up shortly after they left the city limits and were not far from the village.

"Did you have a nice nap, Joshua?" Vivian asked.

"Yes, I guess I did. I must have been tired."

"Marguerite wanted to come tonight, but she had to do her homework," Vivian continued.

"Marguerite is a nice girl. She is very kind and thoughtful," Joshua said in a sleepy voice as if he were starting to drift off again.

"My husband and I are both glad the two of you are good friends. We always worry about the kinds of people our children hang out with. We are so happy your family moved into our village. I love your mother. She is so sweet, and always so gracious. I have never met a woman quite like her. She is really down to earth, but she is so gentle and refined. I would have thought she was raised in a palace, or came from a well-to-do family."

"We are just simple people, as my father always says. I suppose my mother is the way she is because she has such respect for others. I think that's why she's so gracious with people. She sees everyone as special."

"What beautiful ways your family has! So different from the way most people are. What a happy world it would be if we were all like that," Bill interjected. "I really like your father. He's a real man. It seems he can do just about everything. All the men in town are talking about him. It's too bad he doesn't socialize and get to know more people. Do you know if he bowls?"

"Bowls? What's that?" Joshua asked, as he had never heard of that before.

Bill laughed and tried to explain, but Joshua could not visualize what he was talking about, so he ended by asking Joshua to tell his father that he would like to invite him to go bowling with him next Wednesday night.

Joshua promised he would. At that point they were at Joshua's house. He thanked the McCabes and got out of the car and, as he reached the front door, he turned and waved good-bye. The door opened and his mother came out and also waved to the McCabes. Vivian opened the car window and called over, "We had a delightful time with your son. He is quite a young man."

"Thank you, Vivian. And thank you both for taking him with you tonight. Can you stop in for a minute?"

"Not tonight. Marguerite is home alone doing her homework. She wanted so much to come with us tonight. We'd love to have you over to our place sometime. Let's plan on it."

"I would love to. Thank you again. Good night."

"I am glad I went to see Mrs. Azzam, Mother. She is such a nice lady. She was so happy and surprised when I walked in. I kissed her on the forehead and asked my Father in heaven to bless her and, if it was his will, to heal her so she could go to her great-grandson's graduation. And I know my Father in heaven always hears my prayers."

Miriam smiled at her son's simplicity and simple faith. She was happy that he had such a tender relationship with God. It made her feel she was fulfilling the commitment she had made to God.

"Joshua, do you have all your homework done?" she asked.

"Mother, I only had computer homework today, and I did that in school. I had a free period and spent some time after school. I am having fun with the computer. It is amazing all the things you can do with it. I'll show you someday."

"I am glad you are having so much fun in school."

"I like to learn. I especially like to learn about all the beautiful things in the world. The world is so beautiful, but it makes me sad when people damage the beautiful treasures my Father in heaven has placed in creation. Mother, where's Father?"

"He was very tired, so he went to bed early. He was wondering if you wanted to go fishing again tomorrow."

"Yes, I would like that. I'll rush home right after school so we will have plenty of time. What are you drinking, Mother?"

"Raspberry juice that I made earlier in the summer, when the bushes in the back were filled with raspberries. It's delicious, and I was just going to pour some for you."

The two sat down at the kitchen table and chatted while they drank their juice. When they finished, Joshua kissed his mother good night and went quietly up to bed.

16

T HE NEXT DAY, JOSHUA COULDN'T WAIT UNTIL school ended. He liked school, but he liked fishing with his father even more, so he raced home as fast as he could and helped Joseph ready the boat and wagon for the trip down the road.

This time Joshua was determined to catch a fish. Last time he had the oddest feeling that his Father in heaven was having fun, playing tricks on him, when he hooked the burlap bag full of soda and beer cans while Joseph caught the big fish. He was beginning to realize that his Father in heaven liked to have fun, too. That was a new experience for him. Maybe this time he would do better.

"Abba, I know I'm going to catch a fish this time. I hope you get one, too."

"Well, good luck, Son. I hope you do catch one. I hope we both do. That would be a nice surprise for your mother."

The water on the lake was not as calm as last time. Because it was later in the fall, the winds were getting stronger, and the water was a little rough for fishing. The lake was deep, however, and they had a good chance of getting larger fish in the deeper water.

Fishing takes patience. Joseph was a very patient man, but Joshua, he was different. Joshua was impatient. Life was a new experience at every turn, and each new experience was full of excitement. There were so many things he wanted to do each day. Waiting for something to happen, even for a fish to find bait, was not something Joshua had a lot of patience for. He was learning that there were some things that he thought he would enjoy, but when he worked at them, he found they were not things he would want to do very often. They were too boring.

After two hours, Joseph had caught two good-sized fish, one a trout, the other a bass. Joshua had done better than last time, but his fish, a bluegill, was just legal size, nothing to boast about. When they went over to Mr. Lockhart's house afterward to give him one of the fish, Joshua did not have the heart to even show him his, or he might have taken it, just so the boy could boast to his mother and his friends at school that he had caught one of the other two big fish. But Joshua was not a phony, and he wouldn't do something like that anyway. He had no problem telling others that his father had caught two big fish and all he got was a little bluegill.

The old man was happy to get the fish. He invited the visitors to sit down for a minute and talk with him. He hadn't seen a soul in almost a week. The only one who regularly came by was the mailman, and Joshua, every couple of days, to see if he needed anything.

Luckily, Jeremy had earlier baked some gingerbread, which was cooling on top of the stove, so he had something to share with his guests. He brightened up when he remembered it and asked if they had ever had real homemade gingerbread.

"No," Joseph answered, "but it smells good."

The old man placed the bread on the table and cut a few slices and placed them in a dish and put out a tub of butter and some currant jelly he had made earlier in the spring. Water was boiling on the stove, so he was ready to make tea if they liked that.

"Miriam has us drinking tea a lot lately. That will be good."

"I am always glad to have someone visit. It's not very often, and I like to have something ready to offer them. I am glad I baked that bread today, especially since you are so good to me. I have found in my long life that there are two kinds of people: people who like to give, and people who like to receive. You two, and Miriam, are people who like to give, and I am so glad to have something to share with you today. Just knowing that you come to visit every now and then brightens my life and gives me something to look forward to."

"Thank you, Jeremy," Joseph responded. "We enjoy visiting with you, and you're very kind to let us fish in your pond."

"That's nothing. I'm glad, and I even benefit from it."

"This bread is delicious, Mr. Lockhart," Joshua commented after smothering the gingerbread with jam and finishing his first bite.

"I'm glad you like it, Son."

"I'll be over to rake the rest of your leaves tomorrow."

"You don't know how grateful I am for you doing that, Joshua. I used to do it, but I no longer have the strength. I wish you would take something for all that work you do. It saves me a lot of trouble."

"I don't need anything, Mr. Lockhart, and you're such a nice man, I'm happy when I can help you. That is reward enough for me."

After finishing their bread and tea, Joshua and his father sailed back across the lake and continued on home.

"I don't know why I can't catch a fish, Abba. And you got two giant ones," Joshua complained to his father.

"The fish must know you're a young one, so the young fish come to you."

"Well, then what did the tin cans think I was last time when they came to me?" Joshua quipped with a grin.

Joseph laughed out loud at his son's quick humor.

"That was good, Joshua. I'm glad you can laugh at yourself. That's important in life. It's sad that some people can't laugh at themselves."

"Well, it *is* funny, Abba. We did have fun today. Mother will be glad that we will have nice fresh fish tonight. I don't know what mine will taste like."

"I don't know, either. I never had that kind before, but we'll find out tonight."

Miriam was sitting on the front porch waiting for them. She was wearing a light green colored shawl to protect her from the cool autumn air that was settling on the village.

"I see you're bringing home supper. Looks like Joshua caught a prize this time, too."

"Not much of a prize, Mother, but enough for a bite each so we can see what it tastes like. I guess father is a better fisherman than I am."

The trout was big enough to roast whole. Joshua insisted on preparing his own. Joseph suggested he fillet it and take out the skeleton. Joshua tried to but didn't do a very good job. He did get two nice fillets, and his mother suggested he fry them lightly in a frying pan with a little olive oil. They didn't turn out badly. And to everyone's surprise they tasted good, with a little salt and fish seasoning added. Joshua was proud of himself. He was learning and he liked that.

What was really on his mind all day, and he couldn't wait to get to it, was his new computer book. He had brought home a library copy so he could read it before he went to bed. The computer fascinated him, and he wanted to learn everything he could about it and be able to do whatever could be done with a computer. So as soon as he finished supper, he went up to his room and started reading. He was amazed that he could learn so much about almost any question he asked a search engine. He laughed at all the funny names they gave everything like Google and Yahoo. He couldn't wait to look up "bluegill" at school the next day.

When his mother passed his room on her way to bed, she knocked and stopped in his room. He was still reading.

"Good night, Joshua. And don't stay up late reading. You're a young boy and you need your sleep."

"I'll read just a little longer. Father and I had fun today. I'm glad we are friends. Some of the kids in school don't have nice relationships with their parents. That's sad."

"You're a lucky boy, Son. Your father loves you very much, and he is just as happy that you are both such good friends."

"You're my friend, too, Mother, but women are different. I just love you, Mother, but you're still my friend, though I can't imagine going fishing with you or playing baseball or football. Friendships with girls are different. Girls are a lot different, and they sure are hard to figure out. It's hard to explain, isn't it?"

"I guess it is, Son. But I love you, and there are things we can do together. We can cook together and bake nice things, and make jelly."

"Some of those things I like, especially cooking, but I think I like baseball and football better."

Miriam kissed him good night and he stood up and kissed her and gave her a big hug.

"Good night, Mother. And I love you. That's more than friendship. You are everything to me."

"And you are to me, Joshua, more than you will ever know."

A tear rolled down her cheek as she left and went to her room.

The next day at school Joshua found out some things that troubled him. A rumor was circulating through the school that three children in another class had been expelled for bringing drugs into the school. They belonged to very nice families, and everyone was shocked. Joshua asked Jimmy if he had heard anything or knew anything about it.

"No, Joshua. I've been keeping away from anything like that since you helped me. Even my parents have changed. It is so peaceful around the house now. I did see some strange cars, and strange people, coming into town recently, and I sort of suspected they were up to something. I saw a car stop. There were two men in it. They talked to two separate older kids walking by themselves."

"That's what they usually do. They don't talk to kids in groups. They single out kids who are alone and work with them individually. This way there are no witnesses. Then they promise the kids big money if they work with them. Some kids will walk away, but others are vulnerable and fall for it, like I did."

This troubled Joshua. He was very close to his friends, but all the others he cared for as well, even though he might not have had much chance to associate with them. He saw the pain Jimmy went through when he had his problems, and he could feel for the ones who had just been expelled from school. He wasn't familiar with them, but maybe he should get to know them and try to help in some way.

So by the end of the day, after shrewdly talking to his friends, he was able to find out the names of the students who had been expelled. By the end of the week he had befriended them and won their confidence. It might not have been the most prudent thing for him to do, because some in town were starting to think he was part of them, and people were starting to talk. Word got back to him, and from then on he was much more careful. He would have to do things differently this time. This situation was much more complicated than the one involving Jimmy and his friends. It was also much more dangerous. Besides that, he did not want to cause his parents a lot of unnecessary worry.

His day was normal, with nothing unusual happening. He kept his eyes and ears open, and learned all he could.

He still spent time with his friends playing football when the weather was nice. He liked football because he could play rough but still not really hurt anybody. Most of the time they did not wear uniforms when they played, and this exposed them to serious injuries.

On one occasion when they were playing their own choose-up game, one of the boys was hurt right after kick-off. Both teams rushed toward each other when the ball went flying down the field. When the two teams met at midfield, one boy was banged up bad by two heavy players on the opposite team. The boy didn't move, and when the others tried to help him, there was no response. They were all scared and didn't know what to do.

Joshua suggested they all get together and pray for the boy.

"What's that gonna do?" one boy asked. Some of the boys laughed.

"God always hears our prayers," Joshua countered very seriously.

"I think we have to get a doctor," another boy said.

"We don't need a doctor," Joshua insisted. "Trust me, just pray with me."

Reluctantly, they bowed their heads and Joshua prayed in a low voice as he talked to his Father in heaven, asking him to make their friend better. "Father, you always hear our prayers. Please bless our friend who has been hurt. Protect him from harm, and make him better."

Everyone answered "Amen."

Then everyone watched the boy. For a moment nothing happened, but then he opened his eyes and sat up.

"What happened to me?" he asked.

"You were hurt and God just made you better," one boy said.

"Yeah, it was freaky. You blacked out and you wouldn't wake up. We prayed for you and you got better. And that was the first time I ever prayed, and it worked."

"Yeah, it really did work," one of the others said.

"Do you feel all right?" Joshua asked him.

"Yeah, I feel great, like nothing happened."

"Should we keep on playing?"

They continued the game and played for another half hour. Joshua's team lost, but they all had fun. At about five o'clock they quit so they could get home for supper.

Toward the end of the game, the policeman, Sergeant Spaulding, who had arrested the previous drug dealers, was standing on the sidelines watching the game. As the other boys were walking away, Joshua walked over and talked to him.

"The boys who got expelled from school, they are not going to get into trouble, are they, Sergeant?" Joshua asked him.

"They're in trouble already."

"I know, but I mean, they won't have to go to jail, will they?"

"No, but we have to watch them for their own protection. We still don't know who's supplying them, so when we find out, we'll spring our trap."

It made Joshua feel better to know that they would be able to catch the dealers. However, it didn't turn out that way. The suppliers found out that the boys had been arrested. As a result, they were more careful than ever, making sure their meetings would be secret.

THE NEXT DAY IT RAINED ALL DAY. JOSHUA TOLD his parents he wanted to stay after school and work in the library. He had been so busy with other things after school, he had not been able to spend the time he wanted on the computer. So this would give him a chance to catch up. He was excited by what he could do on the Internet and all he could learn about anything he wished. The word "Google" made him chuckle every time he saw it. What a funny name for a search engine! But Google did what he wanted it to do, and he was happy with it.

He wanted to learn all he could about drugs and where they came from, and what groups were involved, and how the drugs found their way into the country. It shocked him to find out that it was like an international army of criminals that was little by little taking control over whole countries and corrupting officials, even high elected officials. Although in his child's mind he did not understand everything, he could grasp the immensity of the evil that these criminals were spreading throughout his Father's creation. It overwhelmed him.

When the librarian walked over to where he was working, she asked him what he was studying so intently. She was shocked to see that he was learning all about drugs.

"Why are you interested in that stuff, young man? You don't want to learn about those things. They're dangerous."

"I'm curious because I know how much damage they do to my friends, and I want to learn all I can about them."

"You sure are an unusual boy, so intense at such a young age."

Joshua cringed every time someone said he was unusual or different or not like the other boys, so he tried to explain that he really was like them, "I just like to learn. I have fun, too. I went fishing the other day in a fishing boat my father and I made. We had a lot of fun. And yesterday I played football with my friends, so I'm not always intense like this, but I want to learn. I enjoy learning. It opens up new worlds for me."

"You're a good boy, Joshua, even if you are different. All the teachers like you, and so do I."

"Thank you, Miss Fletcher. You're a nice lady, too, and I thank you for letting me stay in here for such a long time to work on the computer. We don't have one at home. They cost a lot of money."

Joshua left just before five and was home in plenty of time for supper.

On the way home, he noticed that the trees all throughout Shadybrook had completely turned color. The streets were lined with red and purple and orange and pink foliage. It was like magic. The cold air the night before had transformed the whole village. It was breathtaking. Looking back up on the mountainside behind the village, he imagined the whole hill was on fire.

He liked the autumn. It was different, but it was sad because he knew everything was dying. He knew it would come back to life, but not before a cold winter when the cold and snow would shut down their whole little world and lock everyone inside for months. But, he thought, winter is pretty too, when all becomes a snowy wonderland.

Rushing home, he couldn't wait to see what his mother had cooked for supper.

"Something smells good, Mother. What is it?"

"Something special, Son. We used to have it a lot, and I had a craving for it. And your father likes it, too."

"It smells so good, and it's cold outside. I can't wait to eat something hot. You made homemade bread, too. I can smell it."

"I wanted that to be a secret, but it's impossible to keep fresh-baked bread a secret."

"Where's Father?"

"He's upstairs resting."

"Is he sick?"

That was a recurring worry for the boy, his father being sick, and the fear that something was going to happen to him. Even though he trusted his Father in heaven, he did not always understand his Father in heaven's plans, and even when he talked to him, his answers were not always clear. It wasn't that he didn't trust God, because no one trusted him the way that boy did. He always trusted his Father in heaven to bring good ultimately, but the way to that ultimate good was not always easy to foresee, or easy to understand or accept.

"Is he sleeping, Mother? Is it okay if I go up and see him?"

"Yes, Joshua, but if he's sleeping, let him sleep. Don't wake him up."

"I won't."

Joshua quietly peeked into his father's room. Joseph was sleeping, but the footsteps woke him, and he told the boy to come in and sit down on the bed.

"Father, are you all right?"

"My dear son, you worry so much. Your Father in heaven watches over us; you have to trust him."

"I do, Abba, but I don't always know what he's up to, especially about you, and it makes me worry."

"Don't worry, Son. God takes good care of me."

"I know, but I can tell you don't feel well sometimes. When I pray for others, they always get better, like Mrs. Azzam, and the boy who was hurt yesterday when we were playing football. But when I pray for you, you don't get better, and that's why I worry. And my Father in heaven doesn't tell me everything. I don't know what I'd do if anything ever happened to you. You're my best friend."

With that, he leaned over and put his head on his father's chest. Joseph put his arm around him and said tenderly, "And you are my best friend, Joshua. My whole life is for you. That is the way your Father in heaven intended it to be. So, don't worry, Son. He takes good care of both of us, and your mother, too."

Joshua fell asleep with his head resting on his father's chest. When Miriam walked upstairs a few minutes later, she saw the two of them sound asleep.

"How beautiful!" she thought as tears flowed down her cheeks.

"How beautiful you are, O God! You fill our lives with goodness and love, and surround us with angels to care for us. While we have little, we are rich, for we have each other's love. Sometimes when we have nothing, you provide for us still what we need each day. Your blessings are overflowing. Your plans for us are full of wonder, as we see how you touch our lives and the lives of all we meet. When we contemplate your ways, they are hard to understand, but when we see how they unfold, we stand in awe at the tenderness of your love."

Miriam often prayed like that, just like she had at the beginning, when the angel first appeared to her.

She kept the supper warm until the two woke up and came down the stairs, full of apologies for being late. She smiled and told them how beautiful it was seeing them asleep. They both blushed.

"We were both tired, dear."

"And we shared, too, Mother."

"Well, let's sit down and eat before it gets cold. Joshua, would you pour the water, and no tricks this time."

"Mother!"

"Yes, Son, no tricks this time," Joseph said.

"So, Mother's been telling you things, Father."

"Let's stop the chatter and get going here," Miriam interjected to prevent them from going down that road.

After thanking God, Miriam asked Joshua if he had heard anything more about Mrs. Azzams's condition.

"She should be all better, Mother. I prayed for her, and I know my Father in heaven answered my prayer."

"What was wrong with her?" Joseph asked.

"She had cancer that the doctor said had spread to her bones," Joshua said. "I heard the McCabes talking about it on the way to the hospital. The doctors said there was nothing they could do but make her comfortable so she would not be in too much pain. Sometimes I feel as if some doctors don't believe that God has anything to do with people's lives. He watches over everyone.

"If my Father in heaven doesn't want somebody home yet, the worst doctor can't kill him. And if my Father wants to take somebody home, the best doctor can't keep the person here. And I know my Father doesn't want Mrs. Azzam home yet, so she has to be okay."

Joseph smiled, surprised at his son's childlike trust in God. Joshua's certainty of Mrs. Azzam's healing shocked him.

"Is she home from the hospital yet?" Joseph asked.

"I don't know, but if she isn't, she should be home soon."

"Mother, this supper is really good. And the hot gravy is perfect for the cold weather."

"Do you like it? It's something I cooked for your father a long time ago. I should have prepared it more often, since I know he likes it."

"What is it?"

"It's very thin slices of lamb wrapped around feta cheese and spices and then wrapped in grape leaves and baked in thick gravy.

"It's delicious, Mother, but it's very rich. I don't think I can eat more than three or four pieces."

"That's a lot. I'm sure your father will be glad to finish what you can't eat."

"Whatever made you think of making these today, Miriam?" Joseph asked.

"A lady ahead of me at the store ordered lamb and she also bought a package of feta cheese, and it reminded me of long ago, so I thought I would surprise you."

"You sure did. Thank you. They are delicious. I see there are enough for tomorrow, too. Good."

"Joshua, how did you do with your computer today?" his father asked him.

"Good, Abba, I got a lot of work done, and I really learned a lot about how to use the computer to do research, and also how to contact people. I even e-mailed a letter to the president, and said that God is sad about the war and when we kill each other, and asked him why there have to be wars, since so many of God's children are destroyed. There have to be ways to make attractive deals and work out problems. Killing people doesn't solve problems. It merely creates more problems and destroys so many innocent families. I hope he answers."

"Son, are you supposed to be using the computer for things like that?" his mother asked.

"Well, the teacher wouldn't give me an answer when I asked why there are wars, and it is still on my mind, so I thought I would just ask the president."

"Just like that?" his father asked.

"Yes, Abba, it's that easy."

"When you have something on your mind, you don't give up, do you?"

"No, not if it means a lot to me, and war bothers me because I know it pains my Father in heaven to see his children being destroyed as if they mean nothing and can be easily trashed."

Miriam and Joseph said nothing, but their thoughts drifted back to long ago when, on the occasion of Joshua's bar mitzvah, the child stunned the temple scholars with his wisdom and the depth of his questions.

When Joshua went to bed that night, he knelt beside his bed and looked out into the sky. The moon was full and bright. It looked so far away, but his thoughts wandered as he wondered why it did not seem far away to him. "Why do I remember the moon as being so very close, and the stars as just a step away? Why do I have memories of wandering past stars and planets as if I could just reach out and touch them? Father, your creation is full of wonder and majesty. Its beauty sings silent songs of praise to your goodness. Good night, Father in heaven. I love you. Bless all my friends, and even those I have trouble with. And take good care of my father, and my mother, too. I love her so much, but she cries a lot. I worry about them. And please stop the war. And please bless a new friend I met. He is hurting and has a big problem. Help him find peace and to know that you love him. Amen."

18

JOSHUA AWOKE EARLY. HE WANTED TO STOP OVER to see if Mrs. Azzam had come home from the hospital. He knew she was an early riser, and if she was home, she would be up and around. Sure enough, she answered the door. Joshua was as shocked to see her as she was to see him.

"My dear boy, your prayers certainly are powerful. After you prayed for me at the hospital, I began to feel better right away, but I didn't believe I was really better. When the doctor came in the next morning and examined me, he told me there was nothing wrong with me and that whatever I had was no longer there. He had two other doctors check me over and they found nothing, so they decided there was no reason to keep me there. They couldn't get themselves to say it was a miracle, but I know it was."

"God always answers our prayers, Mrs. Azzam."

"But not the way he answers yours, Joshua. Yours are on the fast track. I never saw anything like it. Oh, my dear, come inside here. I was so excited I forgot to invite you in."

"I really can't, Mrs. Azzam. I'm on my way to school. I just stopped to see if you were home yet. I'm so glad you are better."

She thanked him, and he left. As he walked down the street, the woman stood watching him for the longest time, wondering how he knew she was coming home, or was actually home, from the hospital. She had to call all her friends right away and tell them about her cure after Joshua's prayers.

Joshua continued on his way to school, happy that his Father in heaven had answered his prayers for that nice woman. But all during class he kept thinking about working at the computer. He wanted to learn all he could about how it operated and what it could do. In computer class he asked the teacher numerous questions, until the teacher finally had to ask him to hold off for a while so he could finish what he had planned to teach for that day.

After school, Joshua stayed for a while and worked on the computer, which the teacher allowed him to do since he was so impressed with the boy's enthusiasm for his class. He practiced finding things on the Internet and enjoyed researching material about the formation of the universe, which fascinated him. So many things seemed familiar, but he could not understand why he would know about things like that, especially since they had happened billions of years ago. He finished with the computer later in the afternoon, then left the school.

Outside, he was surprised to see Sergeant Spaulding's police car parked near the principal's car. All the other cars were gone. He wondered what had happened to cause the police to talk to the principal. Sergeant Spaulding had probably heard the same rumors that Joshua had.

Walking down the street, Joshua met Marguerite, whom he hadn't seen in a long time.

"Marguerite, I had a nice ride to the city with your mother and father a few days ago."

"I know. They told me all about it. I wanted to go, too, but I had to do my homework. Mrs. Azzam has been a good friend of ours since I was a child. I'm glad she's better. She told my mother and father that she got better because of your prayers."

"God always answers our prayers."

"He doesn't seem to answer my prayers."

"Maybe he thinks the things you pray for are not good for you. God worries about you, you know, and he doesn't want anything bad to happen to you. You are precious to him."

"I wish I could believe that."

"It takes time to understand God. I have a hard time sometimes, too. I think he likes to play games. I think he must have a sense of humor, because I don't think he's as serious as I thought. I'm learning more and more about my Father in heaven, I mean, about God."

"Joshua, you are a strange one sometimes. No one ever talks like you talk."

"But I'm just like everyone else."

"In many ways you are, but you are different. You think differently, and you are so concerned about everybody. And I don't know anybody who thinks about God the way you do. It's as if he's real to you."

"Isn't he real to you, too, Marguerite?"

"Well, yes, I pray to him when I get up in the morning and when I go to bed at night."

"Is that all? I mean, don't you think of him during the day?"

"No, not unless something's happened and I need him."

Joshua didn't say anything, and Marguerite asked him, "Are you all right? Did I hurt your feelings, Joshua?"

"No, I'm just glad I can talk to you like this. And I know you won't share it with anyone else. But, my Father, I mean, God, is always so close to me, I think of him all day long, and I even dream of him at night, and I miss being home. Well, I think I'd better get home. I'm late already. I'm glad I can talk to you like this. You're my friend, and I can trust you."

On the way home Joshua realized he had talked too much, and he hoped that Marguerite would keep it to herself. But once he went into the house, he called his mother. She was in the kitchen preparing supper. She had just taken a pie out of the oven and was wiping her hands on her apron when Joshua came over to her and gave her a big hug and kissed her.

"I missed you, Mother. But I really learned a lot in school today. I also saw Marguerite on the way home. She's a good friend, although I think I said something I shouldn't have."

"What was that, Son?"

"We were talking about God and about praying. She said I was different, and I don't like it when people tell me I'm different. And I asked her if she also didn't talk to God. She said she prays in the morning and at night. When I asked her if she talks to him during the day, she said no. Then I told her that I felt close to God and think of him all during the day, and then I slipped and said something that even shocked me. I said that I missed being home, and I wasn't talking about here. Why would I say something like that? Mother, I got frightened when I said that and told her I had to go home, trying to cover up what I had just said. Why would I say I missed home?"

"I don't know, Son. There are some things you say and do that I don't understand, either. All I know is that you and God are very special to each other, and he is always with you. That's all I know. We are both learning more and more about your Father in heaven. Being close to God is not always easy, Son.

"When God has something special for a person, the way is never easy. There will always be pain when God chooses someone for a special mission, because they are set apart from other people and are never understood. Their training is hard as they are being prepared. Their ways become different and their hearts are pure, and they become more and more strangers to the world. They have to understand that and be strong to endure the pain of being so close to God.

"So your life, Son, will not be easy, either. But always know that God will always be by your side and in your heart, and you will never be alone, even though you will *always* be alone. And don't expect to be understood. You will never be understood, not even by those closest to you."

"Thank you for helping me to understand, Mother. You're the only one I can talk to. You seem to understand what I feel inside. Mother, life isn't easy, is it? I love life, and I have a lot of fun, but there's a lot of pain, too, especially when you feel other people's pain."

As he walked away, Miriam looked at him with compassion and could feel his pain and confusion, so difficult for so young a child to suffer. "He shall be a sign of contradiction, and cause for the rise and fall of many. And your own soul a sword shall pierce." How many times those prophetic words had crossed her memory! She was learning more and more what it meant.

Joseph had been working at the mill and was just coming home. He looked very tired. Joshua met him at the front door and opened it for him.

"Hi, Abba! You worked at the mill today?"

"Yes, Son. One of the men didn't show up, so I took his place. The owner of the mill was there today. His name is Jonathan Azzam. He said the nicest things about you. He said that his mother was cured of her cancer because of your prayers."

"I just prayed for her, Father. God cured her."

"I know, but the family is still impressed and grateful. His mother was so looking forward to going to her great-grandson's graduation. The doctor told her that it would be all right for her to go."

Joseph walked into the kitchen and kissed Miriam, put his lunchbox on the table, and walked upstairs to rest and wash up for supper. Joshua went out into the yard and picked nuts from an old black walnut tree. His mother liked to use them for baking. Joshua liked the challenge of opening them and getting the meat out without breaking the shell into tiny pieces. That was hard, and he was determined to find a way to do it. He had once tried using his father's band saw, and by putting a nut between two pieces of wood he could slide the nut into the saw and cut the nut in half, then turn the nut around and cut more of the shell off. Eventually he cut off enough of the shell to pick out good-size pieces of the meat.

However, that was too slow, so this time he was going to try a different way. He got his father's small sledgehammer, and with that he would not have to bang hard like with a small hammer. The weight of the sledgehammer cracked the shell nicely, then, turning the nut around slightly, he hit it again, and broke a little more of the shell. Finally, the shell was weakened enough for him to pick out big chunks of the meat. By suppertime he had picked a whole big bowlful of walnuts.

"I finally figured out a way to do this, Mother. There's some for you and some for me. They're different. I like them. They're better when you put them in cookies."

"Joshua, you never give up. I'm surprised you found a way to get so many big pieces."

"Where's Father?"

"He went upstairs to rest and wash up. He should be down soon," Miriam replied.

A short time later he emerged, half asleep, and Joshua couldn't wait to tell him about the walnuts.

"I picked some walnuts off that tree out in the back, Abba. I figured a way to crack the shell so I could get big pieces of the meat."

"How did you do that?"

"Well, I used your little sledgehammer and hit the nut gently. The weight of the hammer was enough to cause the shell to crack nicely. Then I turned the nut a little and hit it again and cracked another small section of the shell. Then the third time, the shell was loosened enough to break it open. That's how I was able to get these big pieces."

"Clever, Joshua. You always were persistent."

"Here, Abba, would you like to try one?"

"Well, they have never been my favorite. Let me taste it." Joseph took a bite. "Not bad. It tastes better when you can chew a big piece like this. Though I think they taste better in cookies or cake."

"Joseph, you had better get ready. It's almost time for

supper," Miriam said, reminding him that he hadn't combed his hair or washed up.

"I'll be back down in a second," he said as he walked up the stairs.

"Joshua, would you set the table, and it's chilly tonight so pour the hot tea I have prepared on the stove. Make sure it's hot."

Supper was always a happy time for the three of them, as they shared with each other all that took place that day. Usually there were good things to share; occasionally there was sad news, like the time one of the workers at the lumberyard, Scott, was badly hurt when a pile of lumber slipped off the truck and almost killed him. Fortunately, it didn't fall on top of him or it would have crushed him, but he was still injured.

The manager asked Joseph if he would go to the hospital with him to visit Scott before they went home from work the next day. Joseph felt honored that the manager asked him. During the ride there, the manager shared things with Joseph that he had never discussed with anyone. Joseph listened quietly, and when the man finished, Joseph made a few simple comments, some concerning the family's need to spend more time with him, as they could be growing farther apart without even realizing it. Another suggestion was that his family might need to see more tangible expressions of his affection and appreciation.

When the two arrived at the hospital, Scott was thrilled to see them. The visit meant so much. His family, who had just arrived for the evening, also appreciated their stopping by.

As Joseph was telling the story about his ailing coworker, Joshua was reminded to ask his father if he had made his appointment with the doctor for his own checkup to see if he was all right.

"Son, you worry about me too much. I am all right. Just because I get tired doesn't mean that there is something wrong with me. It's normal when people work hard, especially when they get a little older."

"Father, I still think it's a good idea for you to have a checkup."

"I will, Son. I will, just to put your worrying mind at rest."

After a while, Joshua went upstairs to do his homework. Thinking he was out of earshot, Joseph asked Miriam, "Why does that boy worry so much? He is so close to God, his Father in heaven as he calls him. I can't understand why his trust in his Father in heaven doesn't calm his spirit."

"Joseph, I don't understand it, either. He seems to have such a beautiful relationship with God; you would think it would calm his worrying."

Then a voice came down the stairs.

"I know you're talking about me down there," Joshua called down as he descended. "The reason I worry is because I think Father is not well, and I don't want anything to happen to him. I know my Father in heaven takes care of him, but I think my father on earth doesn't cooperate with him and take care of himself when he doesn't feel well. If he was more concerned about his health, I wouldn't worry. I just hope God doesn't want my father to come home to him for a long time. It would be horrible without him, Mother."

Tears welled up in Joseph's eyes at the tender expression of his son's love for him.

"I promise, Son, I will go to the doctor real soon, so please don't worry anymore."

"Okay, Abba. I'll go do my homework now," he said as he started back up the stairs. "Good night! I love you both."

"Good night, Son," his parents said in unison.

"How can you not love that boy?" Joseph said as he heard Joshua's door close.

19

AT SCHOOL NEXT DAY, JOSHUA FOUND OUT FROM his friends why the sergeant's car was in front of the school the day before. The police had evidence that drug pushers had been in the neighborhood again, but it was a different group this time, trying to recruit kids to hand out sample drugs to their friends in the village. Sergeant Spaulding wanted the principal to ask the teachers to watch for anything unusual, or if they noticed any strange behavior on the part of any of the students to inform him personally.

From Joshua's past experience with his friend Jimmy, Joshua was super-alert to anything like that. He would be more watchful than ever for any kind of strange behavior. He didn't want anything to happen to his friends, and the way he felt toward others, everyone was his friend. He wanted nothing to happen to any of them. He would watch over them like a shepherd boy protecting his sheep.

When it came to this issue, however, Joshua kept everything to himself. As young as he was, he knew he could not be too trusting. He saw how loose kids' tongues were, and how a little slip could be tragic. So he would keep his eyes and ears open, and would, at the proper time, confide in his friend, Sergeant Spaulding, who himself never approached Joshua, knowing it would single him out for others' suspicion.

Sergeant Spaulding sensed that if Joshua knew anything, he would approach him at the proper time, discreetly, in order to protect his young friends, always demanding assurance that nothing would happen to them. For his part, Joshua knew he could trust Sergeant Spaulding to help him protect the kids from harm.

Once out of school that afternoon, he sought out Jimmy to make sure he was okay.

"Hi, Joshua!"

"Hi, Jimmy! How's everything at home?"

"It's so different, thanks to you. My parents have been wonderful. I think they are in love with each other again. And I don't want you to worry about me and this new situation. I'm staying clear of all of them this time. I learned a hard lesson before. So don't you worry about me, Joshua. I'm okay."

"I'm glad, Jimmy. Remember, I'm your friend and you can trust me, so don't be afraid to share with me if anything is troubling you."

"I won't. I promise."

The two walked away from the school and down the street together until they parted ways to go down their own streets.

It was the weekend, and as soon as he arrived home, his mother reminded him that they would be going to the city the next day for religious services.

"Mother, if there's nothing for me to do around the house now, is it okay if I play football with my friends? They asked me this morning, and I told them I would find out when I got home this afternoon."

"Go and have fun, Joshua, but be careful. You're not wearing any equipment, and it's easy to get hurt. That's a rough game."

"Nothing will happen. I'll be careful."

With that, he went upstairs and changed into his old clothes and came running down the stairs and out the front door, telling his mother on the way out, "I'll be home in time for supper, Mother."

"Have fun, Son, and be careful."

"I will."

As soon as he went outside, he met some other friends on their way to play football. Joshua had learned a lot about sports in the short time his family had lived in Shadybrook. Football was one of his favorites. Joshua liked to play hard, and after he had found his running legs, he was fast, so he was a natural as a receiver. His team easily won this choose-up game. Even when his team lost, it never bothered him. He just liked playing with his friends.

During the game he noticed a strange car parked down the road from the field. He glanced over at it to see what was going on and saw five older boys emerge from the woods and approach the car. A man got out and walked behind the car, took something from the trunk, and gave it to the boys, who immediately disappeared back into the woods. The car drove off, passing the place where Joshua and his friends were playing. Trying not to be obvious as he talked to a teammate, he looked over the boy's shoulder and caught the license plate number on the back of the car.

As Joshua walked home after the game he had to pass the village police station, and when he saw Sergeant Spaulding's car parked out front, he decided to stop in.

"Joshua, my little friend! You look like you've been roughin' it up."

"Just finished playing football. We had fun."

"Did you win?"

"We did. I even scored two touchdowns."

"That's great."

"Sergeant Spaulding, I have to tell you something."

"Come into my office, Joshua."

As they were seated, the sergeant smiled and asked him, "Now, what does my young friend have on his brilliant mind today?"

Joshua then proceeded to tell the sergeant what he had seen at the ball field. He said it looked like there was something strange taking place, and that he was afraid for his friends.

"What do you think they were up to?"

"I don't know. But when the boys slipped out of the woods at that place, the car was already waiting for them, so they must have had something arranged beforehand. If what they were doing was honest, wouldn't they have met at someone's house, or on the main street?"

"Good deduction, Joshua. What kind of a car was it?"

"I don't know much about cars, but I did get the license plate number."

The policeman laughed.

"Joshua, you sure are a sharp kid. That is a great help. What's the license number? I'll look it up right now."

Joshua gave the officer the number, and he entered it into his computer right away. In no time, the name and address of the owner of the vehicle appeared on the screen. Joshua looked closely and memorized all the information.

"The car is from out of state. I have the address, and I'll contact the police in that area to see if they have anything on these people. I'll get on this right away, Joshua. But I want you to be careful. These are not just local drug dealers. These guys are big time, and very dangerous."

"I am careful. I just keep my eyes and ears open. I don't want anything to happen to my friends. They are all very innocent, and I don't want bad people to hurt them."

"You're a smart little fellow, Joshua. I don't know where you get your wisdom from. You're perceptive far beyond your years."

Joshua smiled, said good-bye to his friend, and continued on his way home. Along the way, an elderly man, Gil, stopped him. Gil had been a pharmacist, a kind, gentle man to whom the whole community was indebted for all he had done for so many of them. Joshua would always stop and talk to him, and they became friends. Gil had been sitting outside in front of his house, waiting for Joshua to come by. Gil had a grapevine in his back yard, and he had a bag of grapes for Joshua to take home to his parents.

"Thanks, Gil. They will love these. I'll like them, too. We'll have them for dessert tonight. I haven't seen you the past few days. Have you been all right?"

"It was a little chilly outside, so I just stayed upstairs reading and saying my prayers. When you get old and there is no one else, you read and pray, and you know you are not alone. Since my wife died, life is so lonely."

"I pray for your wife since she died even though she's already in heaven. Prayers deepen her happiness in heaven. And I know she thinks of you all the time, and she's never far away. If you could reach out through that veil, you could hold her hand right now."

"Thank you, Son. You are a very special young man."

Joshua thanked him for the grapes, said good-bye, and continued on his way home.

"How was your football game, Son?" his mother asked as soon as he entered the kitchen.

"We had a good game. It was fun," he answered as he kissed her on the cheek.

"Hi, Abba! You worked at the lumberyard today. Are you tired?"

"Everybody's tired after a long day's work. Aren't you tired after your classes and a football game?"

"I am, Abba, and I'm starved, too."

"We have a nice supper, Son, so go and wash up and hurry back down. Supper's almost ready."

Joshua ran up the stairs, two at a time.

"Joshua, that's dangerous. You could lose your balance and fall down backward. Take one step at a time, please," his mother called out to him.

On entering his room, he saw an unusual number of birds outside his window, clamoring for whatever food was in the feeder. Opening the window, he filled the feeder with bread crumbs and sunflower seeds, which he had collected from plants growing in the back of the flower garden. As soon as he closed the window, the birds flew back. One he had never seen before. It was dark blue, not a blue jay, much smaller, and solid blue, unlike the bluebird he was used to seeing occasionally. It was so pretty. He stood by the window and watched it, hoping it would come back again.

"Are you almost ready, Joshua?" his mother called to him.

"Yes, Mother, I'm coming down in a second."

Supper was simple, some leftovers, and meat loaf, which was delicious, made from different meats left over from other meals. Joshua could never figure out how his mother could get such varied tastes from just ordinary food.

"Mother, I am famished, and this is really good, especially after the strenuous football game."

"Your mother sure is creative. I'm glad I don't have to do the cooking. I wouldn't know where to start," Joseph commented.

"See how much we need you, Mother?"

"It's nice to be appreciated," Miriam responded with a blush.

"Do you think we can go for another boat ride before it gets too cold?" Joshua asked.

"It's too cold for me already," Miriam commented. "If you two want to go, feel free to. I'll go with you when the weather gets warmer."

"We could probably go fishing sometime next week, if it doesn't get any colder."

"Could we bring my friend Jimmy with us? I know he would love to go fishing with us."

"That would be nice, Son. We should all have a good time. But, don't forget tomorrow. We are going to the city for our Sabbath services. Next week we can go to church here in the village."

"Joshua, while you were playing football, and while you were at work, Joseph, Mrs. McCabe came over for a visit and told me that Mrs. Azzam had left for her great-grandson's graduation. As old as she was, she was so thrilled to be taking a plane ride. It's the first time in her life that she will be flying."

"That is good news. I hope she has a wonderful time. She was so looking forward to it. She is such a gracious lady," Joshua said.

"Mrs. McCabe said that Mrs. Azzam made her promise to tell you good-bye and to thank you for your prayers, which she still feels is what made her better."

Joshua blushed and put his head down.

"You certainly have a way with all the elderly ladies, Joshua," Joseph said teasingly.

"Abba, they know I like them, and I help them when they need someone. They are so alone, and have no one near. They must be frightened, never knowing what's going to happen to them, and no one to care for them."

"As soon as you two finish, I have a new dessert, home-made ice cream with no sugar and no fat," Miriam told them.

"And no taste either, right?" Joseph added.

"Joseph! No, this is delicious. Wait till you taste it."

Taking the ice cream from the freezer, she served it and, to their surprise, it was delicious.

"Miriam, how did you make this? It *is* good," Joseph admitted.

"With powdered egg whites and no-fat milk and some arrowroot and that new substitute for sugar, Splenda, and vanilla and cream coconut milk, but not much. Then you put it all in the blender and it becomes nice and creamy. It's best if you don't let it freeze, but just keep it slightly soft. You really have to eat it before it completely freezes. It's not the same when you melt it after it's frozen."

"It really is good, Mother. I'll have to watch you next time so I can learn to make it."

After supper, Joshua went to his room to study, determined to master the computer. However, he noticed that something strange was happening. His concentration and the intensity of his focus seemed to cause his mind to play tricks on him. He began to notice that when he asked the search engine for answers to questions, especially about something that took place years ago, his mind often came up with an answer before the computer put it on the screen. Frequently what his mind told him was different from what the computer told him, so he began to have a problem. Which was right, what his mind told him, or what the computer came up with?

In checking matters further, he found that what his mind was telling him was correct, and the computer had the facts wrong. So, he now had two other problems. How did he know about historical events that took place many years ago? And how could the computer be making mistakes?

The answer to the first question he could not figure out. But, in looking into how the computer gets its information, he found out that people have to put the information into it, then others can look up what someone else put into the database.

What the computer was doing, however, was forcing Joshua's mind to develop faster than it would have, and raising more questions for him to worry about, like where did all this unlearned knowledge come from. This was another frightening piece of evidence that he *was* different from others, when he didn't want to be different. But, his mother's words comforted him. He was different because God made everyone different so each person could do the special work God wanted each one to accomplish in their life.

"I wonder what that special work is that my Father in heaven wants me to accomplish?" he said to himself. "I wish I knew so I could start now."

"You are doing that work already, my son," he heard from a voice within.

Putting aside his computer book, he picked up his math book and began to do the assigned homework problems, and some others besides. They were fun because math was always precise and unchangeable, and it kept reminding him that this is the way everything in the universe works, based on mathematics.

Tired from the stress of the day, he put his head on his little study table and fell sound asleep. When his mother passed his room and saw him, she walked over and kissed him on the head and tiptoed out of the room, knowing that he would eventually wake up and get into bed. His father walked in quietly, kissed him, and left.

The next day at school, just before class, Miss Axeman asked Joshua if he would do some special work for her on the computer. The teachers were all talking about how fast Joshua was learning everything about the computer. He was beginning to ask questions even the computer teacher couldn't answer.

"Yes, Miss Axeman, I'd be glad to do work for you on the computer. I've been learning how to type, so I think I can do a pretty good job. It may take me a while because I can't type fast yet, but I don't like to make mistakes, so I correct everything I do, and it takes more time. But if you can be patient with me, I'll be glad to do it for you."

"I'm not in a big rush, but I would like it done within the next couple of days."

"Oh, I think I can do that if it isn't too much work."

"I'll give it to you after class, and you can look it over when you get a chance."

"Okay."

As he walked to his seat, one of the girls who liked Joshua said in a low voice as he passed, " 'Oh, Joshua, can you do some special work for me?' Teacher's favorite little pet!"

Joshua smiled at her and said, "I like you, too."

"That's nice, but you are her little lover-boy."

He just kept going to his desk.

As the day went on and the students passed from one class to another, Joshua noticed that some of them were acting strangely, even some of his close friends. Before the day was out, he knew someone had introduced them to some kind of drugs.

Joshua never missed much. He seemed to notice everything, even more so since his friend Jimmy had his bad experience. It pained him deeply to see his other friends becoming involved, especially now that real professionals seemed to be moving into the village from other places.

The first thing he wanted to do was look for Jimmy, but Miss Axeman called him to her desk and told him what she wanted him to do on the computer for her. But as soon as she told him, he ran out to look for Jimmy to make sure he was all right. He found him right away. Before he could say a word, Jimmy burst out, "Stop worrying, Joshua, I'm all right. I'll be okay. I am so afraid of the stuff, there's no way I will get sucked into it again, thanks to you."

"I feel better. Now you have to be careful, Jimmy, and keep your distance from the ones who are involved. You can become suspect."

"I will. I already know some of my friends are involved, so I go right home after school and do my homework, then call up my other friends. Too bad you don't have a phone in your house."

"I know, but we can't afford one. If you want me, though, just talk to me where you are. I will know."

"Joshua, you are weird. What are you talking about? How can you hear me when you don't have a phone?"

Then Joshua remembered his mother's warning to keep quiet about his special gifts.

"Yeah, I guess it does sound weird. Well, just talk to me anyway if you need me, and we'll see what happens."

"Whatever you say, but I think it's weird."

The two walked part of the way home together, then parted, each going his separate way. Joshua returned to school to work on his project for Miss Axeman.

When he finally left for home, snow began to fall. It was the first for the year. Joshua was thrilled. It was a new experience. He held out his hand to catch the snow as it fell. It melted immediately. He looked at it closely. Each flake was a tiny crystal with a beautiful pattern, and each one was different. He looked up. "Father in heaven, thank you! The snowflakes are beautiful, each one special. You fill our lives with awesome gifts each day, and of most we are not even aware."

By the time he arrived at home, greeted his mother, and went up to his room to see the birds' reaction to the snow, there was already a white ground cover. Birds of all kinds were flittering around his bird feeder, hardly any of them getting a chance to feed because of all the excitement.

When he appeared in the window, they all flew away, then gradually came back one at a time. He sat down on the floor and watched them for a long time. Eventually his mother came up to see what his hurry was to go upstairs. When she saw him, she realized his curiosity and sat down on the floor near him to watch the birds.

"I have never seen so many birds at a bird feeder, Joshua, and there are so many different kinds. Where do they come from?"

"I don't know. I think they just keep looking around for a place where they can get food every day. That's why I don't like to miss putting food out for them. Little by little they came from all over. I love to watch them. They're so beautiful and so full of life, and all so different with different personalities. They are a lot like people.

"Two weeks ago I started putting out some food for the turkeys that wander into the back of the yard. They're funny. I like to watch them. I can tell they can see me even when I try to hide off to the side of the window. They keep watching, and if I make the slightest move, they will start to walk away, then stop and look back. If I don't move, they come back and start to eat, but keep looking up at the window. They are smart.

"One day two mother turkeys came with a whole brood of babies. They ignored the food and brought the babies over into the bushes and walked back out, leaving the babies in the bushes. The two mother turkeys walked out into the open field. I wondered why they left the babies behind, and then I noticed there was a fox farther out in the field near a clump of trees.

"The two turkeys walked right out toward the fox, which started to walk in the opposite direction and then disappeared. The two mother turkeys came back and somehow called the babies, which came from the bushes, and they all ate the food I had put out for them. That was so exciting. I then wondered how they talked to the babies. They must have their own language."

"You really have a lot of fun, don't you, Joshua?"

"Mother, I think life is so full of adventure. We just have to look for it and notice it. I do have a lot of fun just watching things happen. There is always so much excitement going on. It's hard not to become involved."

Miriam had no idea all what her son was thinking when he said that, and he did not explain any further.

"Mother, will you show me how to make that ice cream before Father comes home from work?"

"I still have some chores to finish, but if you come right down, I'll show you. It's not complicated, so I can show you in a few minutes. And when you come down, Son, please come down one step at a time. You're going to break your neck one of these days."

"I already told you I wouldn't do that anymore. And I haven't. So stop worrying. And besides, you know what it says in the psalm, 'He assigns his angels to watch over him, lest he stub his toe against a stone.' "

"Yes, but God expects us to use common sense. I don't see that sometimes. That's why I worry. Please be careful. I often feel that you aren't sharing everything with me."

"Mother, I am always very careful. Even when things are complicated, I can always see ahead what is going to happen, and I do what I have to do, so please don't worry. I always end up telling you eventually, Mother. I really don't keep anything from you. You and I are very special to each other. Our two lives are really almost one. I think that's the way my Father in heaven planned it. What you feel, I feel, and what I feel, I know you also feel."

Miriam said nothing, but a tender, thoughtful look betrayed what crossed her mind, that painful memory of the old priest's prophecy. And it was becoming more and more clear to her that when even as a young child he was experiencing deep pain, he was unable to share completely, thinking to save her from worry. She could sense he could feel the pain and anguish of others around him and could not rest until he could ease that pain. She worried, "Is that what Isaiah meant when he prophesied, 'He carried upon himself the pain of us all.' And is that what his whole life is going to be like?"

By the time Joshua went to bed that night, the temperature had dropped considerably. There was also close to six inches of snow on the ground. Joshua had thought about going to school the next day. He knew he had no warm clothes to wear, but, not wanting to cause his mother concern, he said nothing. But when she saw the weather was not going to change, she knew she had to put something together for her son and husband to wear when they went out in the morning.

Not having any material she could use to make warm coats, she found two blankets that had sentimental value because they were given to her by poor people she had once helped. They were made of very good soft wool.

With a quickly drawn pattern that had a slightly oval shape, she cut both blankets and sewed a hem around the edges, cut a hole in the middle and hemmed it neatly, then put slits in the side and hemmed them. With material left over, she made hoods and attached them to the hole in the center. It was late into the night when she finished. After hanging them up on hangers, she put them on pegs on the kitchen wall for Joshua and Joseph to pick up in the morning. Finally, after the long day and night, she retired.

Next morning, Joshua woke up early, excited to see the snow outside his window and to watch the birds. After talking to his Father in heaven and asking his guidance for the day and help for his parents and all his friends, he went to the window and was thrilled to see the many birds that were flying back and forth from the trees and shrubs to the feeder, eating voraciously. The beautifully colored birds stood out in dramatic contrast to the brilliant snow covering the trees and the ground.

When Joseph woke up and readied himself, he started downstairs and, walking past Joshua's room, peeked in and saw him watching the birds. Even he got excited seeing so many birds feeding all at one time. He walked over and watched them with his son.

"Good morning, Father! Aren't they beautiful?"

"They are, Son. I never realized they could be so much fun to watch. Are you coming downstairs?"

"Yes. I'm going to wash and get ready, and I'll be down in a few minutes."

When Joseph entered the kitchen, he saw the new coats and realized Miriam must have been up half the night making them. He knew she must be tired, so he started making breakfast, so when Miriam and Joshua came down, they would be surprised to know that he really *could* make breakfast.

Even Joshua was surprised when he came down, after smelling the aroma of cooking garlic and onions and olive oil and sausage floating up the stairs. It also woke up his mother, who rushed to get ready after oversleeping.

They all finally sat down for breakfast and laughed out

loud at their surprise over Joseph's delicious breakfast. The two men made a big fuss over their brand-new coats, which they were so surprised to see and couldn't wait to put on.

On the way to school, Joshua met a group of his friends. They were all shocked at the unique clothes he was wearing.

"Joshua, what is that you're wearing?" his friend George McHenry asked. "It's really cool."

"It's special made," Joshua answered. "I don't know what they call it. It's very comfortable and warm. My mother made one for me and one for my father."

"I like the colors, dark red, green, and brown," Jimmy commented. "I wish I had one like it."

"You don't even need gloves with that," Charlie added. "You can just put your hands underneath and keep them warm, then put them through the opening when you have to use them."

"I like the hood," Joshua said. "It's so snug and warm."

"Oh, and Miss Axeman will say, 'Joshua, you look so cute in your new outfit,'" Marguerite commented in a jokingly sarcastic way.

Joshua blushed and laughed.

"See you after school," Jimmy said as he left to catch up with another friend.

"Have fun," Joshua told him.

When Joshua got to his classroom, sure enough, Miss Axeman met him at the door and immediately commented, "Oh, Joshua, you look so cute in your new outfit."

Joshua laughed, then caught himself and said thank you.

"Why are you laughing?" she asked.

"Because someone said outside that you would say that to me."

"Well, you do."

"My mother made this for me last night. She must have stayed up late to do it. She made one for my father, too."

"Your mother is very talented. I wish I could make beautiful things like that."

"It's because clothes cost so much in stores, my mother tries to make our clothes for us."

"Joshua, did you finish the little assignment I gave you?"

"Yes, I did, and I was surprised to learn what I did. I didn't realize that Abraham came from what is now Iraq, from the Chaldean Mountains, so the people in that area are closely related to the Jewish people. I have the printout of the assignment in my folder here," he said as he took the folder and handed it to the teacher.

"Thank you, Joshua. Judging by the number of pages, you did quite a job researching that for me. Thank you."

The bell rang for class and everyone took their seats.

Miss Axeman called the class to order and began the Pledge of Allegiance to the flag. The class continued, that is, all except three students. One student insisted on making a remark about having to mention God in the pledge. Her parents had told her it was a violation of her rights. A boy backed her up and agreed with her. They said they were offended that the class mentioned God. It's like praying to God.

Joshua put up his hand.

"Yes, Joshua, did you want to say something?"

"I'd like to tell a little story."

"Make it short, Joshua!"

"Six people are out on the ocean in a boat. A violent storm comes up and the boat is being thrown about by the wind and the waves, and is filling up with water besides. One of the crew says, 'Let us pray and ask God to save us, or we are surely going to drown.'

" 'I don't believe in God,' two of the people say. 'But if it helps, go ahead. I'll even add my Amen.'

"Isn't it interesting, those two people did not feel offended. And after a short time the storm calmed down, the sky became blue, and the sun came out. But they forgot to thank God, except for one, one of the two who did not believe in God. And now our country is at war and we are in danger, and other children of God are in danger as well. Why should anyone be offended when we ask our Father in heaven to save us? He's the only one who can save us from the trouble that threatens us."

No one said a word, and the teacher, afraid to comment for fear of criticism, immediately began the class.

During the day Joshua noticed that some of the kids were not themselves. Even though they were not his close friends, they were good kids and good students besides, and he could sense they had taken something that was making them act differently. He was hoping the teachers hadn't noticed the change in their behavior so they wouldn't get into trouble. Later in the day he noticed other students from other classes acting strangely. How could there be so many involved?

He was beginning to see that this was not like the last time, when the operation was limited in size. This time it was well organized and could do serious damage to the whole community. But he said nothing. He knew that, under circumstances like this, no one could be trusted. He just watched and listened and made believe he heard and saw nothing. Sometimes it takes rare intelligence to know nothing.

Outside of school afterward, as he was walking with some friends, he casually noticed an older student talking to a younger student and slipping him a little package. The younger kid then put something in the other's hand, and they parted. Of course, Joshua saw nothing, but remembered everything. As the days went on, he saw more and more of this behavior, then began to see much older students in senior high contacting the older elementary school students.

Having an impeccable memory, he gradually learned the names of most of the young people in the village and where most of them lived. He was also beginning to realize that this whole operation was well organized and that the drugs must be being channeled to the little kids by way of the high school students. Who was giving the drugs to the high school students, and where that was being done, was the mystery.

Probably not at the high school, as Joshua knew from hearing the policemen talking that there were detectives watching that school, and that many of its students took the school bus back to the village. There was little chance they were picking up the drugs there. Drop-offs for the local kids were probably being done somewhere around the village. Joshua was more alert than ever, yet he said nothing to anybody, not even to his friend Sergeant Spaulding, with whom he did not want to be seen talking even casually.

"Mother," Joshua said as he walked into the house, "everybody loved my new coat. I love it, too. It is so warm, and it fits perfectly."

"Thank you, Son! How was school today?"

"Good. I had a special assignment from my teacher, and when I turned it in she was impressed and thanked me for it. She wanted me to do some research for her. I did it on the computer, and I learned something very interesting, that Abraham came from what is Iraq today, in the area of the Chaldean Mountains, and that Jewish people and the Iraqi people are family."

"That is really interesting. You learn a lot from that computer, don't you?"

"It's amazing how smart the computer is. Of course, someone has to put all that data, they call it, into the database for others to pick up when they are searching. It's fun searching."

"Joshua, you are like a little ferret. You never give up until you find what you are looking for. That is good, but you don't want to be so focused and so serious that you lose your sense of fun."

"Mother, I will never lose that. I love to have fun too much for that. I find joy and fun in practically everything around me. I just worry a lot about all my friends. Life isn't simple for kids, and I don't like seeing them getting hurt."

"What do you mean, Son?" Miriam asked, knowing she was treading on thin ice, which he would immediately notice and cause him to move on to something else.

"Kids have a lot of problems, you know, problems at home, problems with school, and some kids aren't very smart and they have a hard time learning. Grown-ups don't understand them, so they get punished a lot."

"You mean the students you have been helping with their class work and math homework?"

"You know about that?"

"Yes, their mothers tell me when I meet them on the street. They say they are so grateful to you. They think you're brilliant."

"I try hard and have a good memory. I love those kids who are having a hard time, and I try to help them, Mother. I have to go out now and do some work for some friends. You don't need me, do you?"

"No, Son. Go, do what you have to do, but be home in time for supper."

"I will, Mother."

He kissed his mother on the cheek and left. She realized how shrewdly he avoided explaining completely what he meant by his friends being hurt.

Joshua spent the next two hours shoveling snow for the old-timers in the village. Mr. Ferraro wanted to give him five dollars for doing his sidewalk. Joshua looked at him and said, "No, please, Mr. Ferraro. My Father in heaven rewards me. He sends his angels to watch over me. I feel so honored that I can do this little job for you. That is reward enough. But, thank you anyway."

It was the same everyplace he went. The old folks appreciated having their sidewalks and steps shoveled, and wanted to pay him, but he insisted that he was happy to do it, and that his Father in heaven paid him well by sending his angels to watch over him. He did, however, to respect their sense of pride, have a cup of tea or hot chocolate when they invited him inside.

He enjoyed chatting with them. They had so many experiences in life that they shared with him, it made him realize that, with all their experiences and learning, they were still being cast aside by people and looked upon as just old, with little value for anyone.

He could feel the pain and loneliness of their rejection, knowing from their stories that they were once important people and highly respected. Now they were just old and of no value to anyone, and often a burden to their families. Joshua made them feel important again, just by listening to all they had to tell him. When he left he thanked them, and they looked forward to the next snowfall.

As he was walking home, he saw the car he had reported to Sergeant Spaulding. He watched it as it turned the corner and went toward the same place, at the end of the ball field, just far enough outside the village not to be noticed. He also spotted four high school boys walking down another street that would put them on the opposite side of the little woods, where a path led to where the car was.

It was too late to tell Sergeant Spaulding. He had already left for home. Joshua did not feel safe about telling anyone else, so he continued on his way home, planning his own little strategy.

The next chance came hardly a week later, when another rendezvous took place. This time Joshua was not far from where the boys were to meet the car. Four men got out of the car as soon as the boys arrived. Opening up the trunk, they took out plastic bags containing a number of much smaller bags of white powder. While they were giving the packages to the boys, Joshua suddenly ran from the opposite side of the street, grabbed a bag from the trunk, and started to run with it through the woods.

The high school boys were first to see what had happened and panicked, running in different directions to escape, not knowing who else might be watching. Being older, they had no idea who Joshua was and wouldn't even recognize him if they saw him again, things had happened so fast.

When the men realized what Joshua had done, they started chasing him through the woods. The path was clear and dry, as the snow had disappeared after two days of sunny weather. Joshua had a good head start, but the men's legs were much longer and they began to gain on him. He was still at least a hundred yards ahead, but apparently knew just what he was doing. Hopefully, his strategy would work. When he came to a fork in the path, he got confused as to which one led to where he wanted to go. He said a fast prayer to his Father in heaven and took the path to the right. He didn't dare turn around. He knew they were following and to turn around would slow him. He kept running as fast as his little legs would carry him, but he tripped on a tree root lying above the dirt. Picking up the bag, which he had dropped, he continued on, knowing the men must really be closing in on him. Fortunately, his sports during the summer had helped him greatly gain in running speed. It just might save his life.

One of the men pulled out a gun, intending to shoot the boy. One of the others yelled out, "You damn fool, don't shoot that thing! You'll have every cop in the area coming down here. We can't be far from the street. We're gaining on him fast, so we should be on top of him soon."

Joshua could hear their voices and knew they were a lot closer, but he didn't dare to turn around. Finally he reached the street. It was Mud Puddle Road. The path came out onto the road not too far from the pond. Joshua kept running toward the pond. Was he hoping to run through the woods there and lose the men, or go to the old man's house on the other side of the lake, hoping to hide there?

The men were now not far behind, hardly a hundred feet away. Joshua was only about fifty feet from the pond. As he reached the pond, he ran out onto the ice. The men were only a few feet behind him now. Joshua kept running, farther and farther out. When he had almost reached the midpoint he heard a loud cracking behind him, and men screaming curses. He knew his strategy had worked. Knowing he could walk on the water, he knew he surely could walk on the ice, which was not very thick, especially in the middle. The four men had fallen through the cracked ice into the freezing water, and every time they tried to climb out, more ice would crack. Joshua knew they were trapped.

He couldn't help but laugh at the frantic drug dealers flailing away in the cold water. He put the bag of drugs down on the ice and walked back to the shore, then ran down Mud Puddle Road into the village to tell his friend Sergeant Spaulding about what had happened. He told his friend he would find the men trapped in the pond with cracked ice all around them, with their bag of drugs on the ice, and their car full of drugs at the place not far from where the previous rendezvous had taken place.

The sergeant laughed, but then asked, "How did you know you wouldn't fall through the thin ice yourself?"

"That's a secret. I just knew it wouldn't happen. Now, remember our deal. The kids are not to get into trouble, but I hope you scare the older ones good, so they won't even think of doing anything like this again."

"A promise is a promise, Joshua. Trust me."

Joshua left for home. The sergeant had other officers follow him in their cars, and upon reaching the pond, they found everything just as Joshua had said, with the four men flailing away in the middle of the cracked ice and the bag of drugs not far from them, but just out of their reach.

After reading the men their rights, the officers pulled them out of the water, handcuffed them, put them in their cars, and drove them to the police station to book them and lock them up. They then impounded the car and, after opening the trunk, they found it just as Joshua had said. It would be hard for the men to get themselves out of this mess, even with the best of lawyers. The only hope they could have would be to plea bargain and hope for leniency if they helped the police dismantle the whole operation.

As soon as Joshua arrived home and walked into the kitchen, his mother looked at him and knew immediately that something had happened. This time she demanded that he tell her.

"Mother, I can tell you everything, but please let me go

and take a shower. I'm tired and nervous, and the hot water will help me feel better. I'm sorry I kept so many things from you, but I had to. I didn't know what I could say or how I could say it. Now it's all over, and I'm finally at peace. But please let me take my shower and I'll tell you the whole story."

"I can't wait. You don't know how I worried. I knew that something was happening, but not knowing what it was was unbearable."

By the time Joshua came back downstairs, his father had come home and they were both waiting for him to come and tell them what had happened. It didn't take him long, and he was honest and straightforward. He could tell they were both deeply troubled that he had gotten so deeply involved in a matter that could have ended in tragedy. When he finished, they praised him for his loyalty and caring for the children in the village, but in his innocence he could have been killed.

They made him promise that he would never again do anything so dangerous and imprudent. After trying to defend why he did it, they insisted that it was not something a young boy should ever become involved in. He was just fortunate that nothing terrible happened, and that he didn't get killed. "Your Father in heaven has given us a heavy responsibility to protect you. And out of love for your Father in heaven, you must follow what we tell you," Joseph told him sternly.

"Yes, Father. I realize now I shouldn't have done it, but I felt it was important to protect my friends and save them from evil."

"You have to leave serious matters like that to the proper authorities. That is not your business," Joseph insisted.

"Yes, Father." And this time he meant it, and realized it was foolish of him to even think of doing such a thing, and especially in not letting his parents know about it. He could understand why it would be very difficult for them for a long time to trust him to make decisions on his own. And that bothered him more than anything, realizing that he couldn't be trusted to be careful, even of his life.

He made it a point after that to be very honest whenever he left the house and to be sure to tell his parents precisely what he was going to do. He knew they trusted him to be honest and truthful, and after a time the tension and worry passed and peace again settled on their little family.

21

WHEN THE ICE ON THE POND MELTED AND spring came, all the heaviness of winter passed. Joshua was a year older and had learned even more about himself and about the remarkable insights he had into the wonder of life itself. He was also learning how precious was each human being to his Father in heaven, and no matter how troubled or crippled in mind or body a person was, they were still loved by God and needed understanding and help from other members of his Father's family on earth.

Destroying one of his Father's children as worthless and disposable struck him with horror. There was no one beyond redemption. In his own quiet and now much more prudent way, Joshua reached out to those he saw who needed help and tried to get them to change their ways.

When the school year ended, Joshua had done well, and all his classmates passed, even those he had quietly helped who never expected to pass. It was a first for some of them, and they were grateful to Joshua. With their renewed and restored self-image, they did well on their own after that year.

Joshua's teachers were proud of his accomplishments. Some teachers knew he was bright; some even thought it was their exceptional teaching ability that was really responsible for his excellent work. Joshua thanked all of them for everything they had done to help him learn and grow.

That summer was exceptionally pleasant. Joshua spent much of the time doing work around the yard and caring for the flower and vegetable gardens, and also playing sports with his friends. Miriam had made many friends in the village, most of them from the poorer families. Many others still looked upon the simple family on Mud Puddle Road as simple poor people, and to those they never became socially acceptable. Only a rare few ever invited them to their homes for social occasions. The poor loved them because they felt proud to be considered one of them. Whenever they had cookouts or parties, Miriam and Joseph and Joshua were always invited.

Toward the end of the summer, Miriam could see that her husband's health was beginning to fail, as he would show signs of fatigue after working only a short time. Perhaps her son was right when he worried about him not being well. The doctor advised her that her husband's heart was weak due to stress over a long period of time. The cold winter weather was not conducive to healing such a condition, and Joseph's doctor strongly recommended that they spend a good part of the winter in a place where the weather is warmer.

Joseph and Miriam discussed the doctor's suggestion, and Joseph had to admit that he had not been feeling all that well over the past year. In fact, just the *thought* of getting a good rest felt healing. But where would they go? Joseph, and even

Joshua, had put so much of themselves into fixing up the house, it made him sad to think of leaving it and all the nice friends they had made here over the past year. However, as reluctant as they were, they made plans to move.

Knowing they had to inform the landlord of their plans, they contacted Mr. Jenkins and made an appointment to meet with him. He said he would come out to Shadybrook and discuss the matter with them. When he arrived, they hardly recognized him. He had grown much older in a very short time and did not look at all well.

When he got out of his car and walked to the house, Joseph went out to help him up the stairs and bring him into the parlor. It was close to noontime, and Miriam had already planned to invite Mr. Jenkins to have lunch with them. In the meantime, they chatted in the parlor for a few minutes. The landlord looked all around and commented on how beautiful everything looked. He asked if he might see the kitchen, and perhaps some of the rest of the house, if they didn't mind.

"Not at all," Joseph said as he conducted him into the kitchen. He looked around each of the rooms Joseph showed him, expressing approval at the excellent workmanship. Miriam and Joseph did not know what to say. They were in mild shock. Looking out at the deck and the back yard, the man could not help but compare what he saw with memories of what it had looked like previously.

"I cannot believe the transformation. It is truly remarkable, and to think I had such a bad attitude about you people when you first told me you needed a place to live. I badly misjudged your simplicity. Where is that boy of yours, by the way? I was hoping I could see him again. I have heard nothing but charming things about that boy.

"My grandson, whose family I have never been close to,

lives in the village here. I have to visit them really soon before it is too late. The boy is a good friend of your son, Joshua. A police officer told me Joshua saved the life of my grandson. After the officer told me the story, I felt so guilty for having abandoned my own flesh and blood that I started doing a lot of soul-searching. My grandson's name is Jimmy Cronin."

Joseph and Miriam were totally taken aback by the shocking disclosure. They knew Joshua and Jimmy were friends, but didn't realize that their son had saved the boy's life, and in the process had completely changed the life of the grandfather. This explained why he was being so gracious. Then they wondered if Joshua knew somehow that Jimmy was related to this man, and if it was Joshua's way of touching this man's heart. There were so many things they did not know about their son. Each day brought new revelations.

"Yes, I would like very much to see that young boy. I should have known when I first saw him that he was a special child, but then I was blind, and it took me a long time to see and understand. Also, being sick was a blessing in disguise. One learns a lot during times of serious illness."

The man did not describe his sickness, but it must have taken a great toll on him. The physical effects were obvious. The psychological and emotional effects, and possibly the spiritual effects were graces from God.

The lunch Miriam served was light, and they continued talking about many things. One of the things was the disposition of the house after the family moved. The man had decided that he would make the house a memorial to Joshua's family in recognition of the goodness they had brought to the community in the short time they had lived there.

He intended also that the house be used in the future to aid worthy individuals in extraordinary need. A foundation would be established to assure the proper use of the house and grounds, and also the extensive field behind the house that Mr. Jenkins also owned. This would assure the permanent use of the property for humanitarian purposes.

By the time they finished talking, Joshua walked in and abruptly stopped when he spotted the man. His memories were still vivid. But he was polite. He said hello, and the man stood and reached out to shake his hand.

"Young man, I am so sorry for being so mean to you. I have learned much about you over the past year, and I also know that you and my grandson are good friends."

Joshua smiled.

"You know that Jimmy is my grandson?" the man asked when he saw the smile of recognition on Joshua's face.

"Yes, sir. I knew that all the time."

The man broke down and cried.

"And you still befriended him, and saved his life. And my life, too, I should add. You are truly a blessed child. There is no way that I can thank you for what you have done, and for all you have done for this community. Your parents will tell you of a little token of my appreciation that I have made in honor of you all. It is my inadequate way of saying thank you, and of saying I am sorry for having been so rude."

"There is no need to apologize, Mr. Jenkins. Understanding comes hard for all of us," Joshua replied. "I just learned that I have a lot to learn yet. It is painful to learn that I still make mistakes. It is even harder to say I'm sorry." He looked at his parents when he said that, aware that they knew what he meant.

As he was leaving, Mr. Jenkins said the whole village would miss them, and certainly his grandson Jimmy. Then he got into his car and drove off.

It didn't take long for word to get around the village that

the family was leaving. There were mixed feelings. Some who had never grown beyond their original prejudice against this poor family were glad at hearing the news. Other people who knew them, especially the elderly and the poor whom the family helped, were devastated. Marguerite and her Joshua admirers were brokenhearted and asked Joshua if he would e-mail them. This he promised to do.

The boat that Joseph and his father made they gave to Jimmy and George, as they were Joshua's closest friends. They would also be the most willing to share the boat with their other friends and were the most interested in boating and fishing. But the boat had to be kept at old Jeremy's dock in case he needed to use it to get to the village or just to go fishing. The little trolling motor went with it as well as the sails and whatever other gear was part of it.

A couple of days before the day of departure, Sergeant Spaulding invited Joshua and his parents to the police station, where the captain presented Joshua with a special medal they had struck in recognition of his dedication to the community and his care for all the young people. They named him "protector of the village." Joshua accepted it proudly. His parents were especially proud, even though they still had reservations about what he had done.

When the day came for the family to leave, they took very little with them, as their possessions were few: Joseph's tools, Miriam's small portable sewing machine, and a bag of clothes for each of them. That was all they possessed on this earth. When they climbed onto the bus, the whole village was there, even those who were glad to see them leave. But even they cried when they finally realized what they had missed during that short, blessed visit.

Some may wonder at the strangeness of this story. "God doesn't work like that," they might say. But who can limit what God can do or cannot do, or limit God to space and time? God is eternal. He is ever present. His life on earth was a process he began when he first came. That process still continues, and will continue until the end of time.

At various times in human history, different aspects of Jesus' life have had special meaning and given special lessons. Today, with life so complicated, it is confusing for young people. They need more than ever to see the beauty of Jesus' life of caring and simplicity and gentleness against the attraction of violence and vengeance.

At various times in history, Jesus appeared in various forms. To Saint Anthony he appeared as a child. To Saint Augustine, trying to understand the mystery of the Trinity, Jesus appeared as an infant shoveling sand out of a hole and trying to fill it with water from the sea. Augustine told him that that was impossible, to which the Child replied, "Not as impossible as trying to absorb God into the human mind." Augustine got the point and approached his contemplation of the Trinity with more humility.

The presence of God in the world is real. Simple, humble people, sensitive to the presence of God in their lives, more readily recognize when he is close and can hear the quiet voice within as he touches their lives. Some, educated beyond their intelligence, see God only in themselves and recognize the real divine mystery often too late. Sophisticated religious people laugh condescendingly at the simplicity of the humble and their beliefs, who are most often the ones with whom God feels most comfortable. Throughout history, they have been the ones whom God has visited, and he gave them messages to share with the rest of the world.